House of Thirteen

Book One

Andy Lockwood

Woe be upon anyone who steals, or borrows and does not return, this book from its owner. May ink from the page stain the thief's hands, marking them for all to see. Let the ink burn, words marking their skin for all time. Let bookworms crawl under their fingertips, burrowing a home where they will gnaw like guilt and shame.

Also by Andy Lockwood:

Empty Hallways

At Calendar's End

Threshold

This is for you, mom.

Of all the gifts you have given me, and all the lessons shared, I think I cherish the weirdness most of all.

I love you.

"Character cannot be developed in ease and quiet. Only through experience of trial and suffering can the soul be strengthened, ambition inspired, and success achieved."

- Helen Keller

PROLOGUE

It was a beautiful day, even if it was the dead of winter.

January had finally decided to grace the sun-starved people of the northern climes with a few hours of their beloved light source. After crushing their spirits with a full week of cloud cover and drifting snow, a few hours was a welcome reprieve.

When it peeked out from behind the clouds just before noon, the streets filled with people looking as though they forgot the sun ever existed. Ren rolled her eyes at the lookie-loos and the gawkers and considered herself lucky she remembered her sunglasses. As much as she appreciated the warmth it brought, the intense reflection off the frozen landscape was less than enjoyable.

She strolled the sidewalks, dancing around man-made moguls and teetering somewhere between not slipping on the ice and trying not to clobber the other pedestrians along the walkway. The tread on her boots didn't seem to give her as much traction as she expected it to. She scrunched up her face in dismay and mentally calculated how many paychecks it would take to get a new pair. As she carried ones and multiplied by sales tax, her sense of responsibility tacked on a few odds and ends that she knew should be handled first. She audibly cursed, realizing there were far too many things standing between her and a new pair of boots.

She reached into her pocket, fishing her phone out as she began scanning and skipping through her playlist. She needed something that could squash her suddenly sour mood. Today was going to be something special; she felt it. She adjusted her ear buds and turned up the volume, her eyes glued to the display on her phone as she barely dodged strangers moving in the opposite direction.

No, no, no.

She clicked through with frenzy, needing only the first couple beats to know if the song was going to fit her monumental day.

No, no – wait.

She backed up one track. The chords danced happily in her ears, the beat racing down to her feet almost immediately. It was the perfect anthem for her day – except for one strange sound that didn't belong. She listened harder, trying to place the sound, oblivious of the city bus bearing down on her.

ONE

At some point between the concrete and the blinding pain that followed, Ren's body could take no more. She simply shut down. She fought for consciousness, feeling herself trapped under the ice and pounding helplessly against the frozen surface. Each time she broke through, she felt glowing warmth radiating from within her. Though she tried to hold onto that warm glow, the pain returned shortly after, an invisible hand shoving her back down beneath the surface of consciousness.

She had no recollection of where she was or what was happening, but each time she woke, she was aware that something had changed around her. Each time, her surroundings had altered. Then she awoke to nothing, just darkness. She was confused, disoriented, and fearing blindness. She wanted to cry, but her body wouldn't obey her.

That's when she realized she couldn't move. Not just that, but she didn't seem to be breathing either. She couldn't even detect her heartbeat in her chest. Panic was starting a storm in her brain. Her fear of blindness had escalated to a fear of paralysis. Or worse, coma.

Then out of the silence, she found stimulus: from somewhere in the shapeless dark, she could hear voices. It was a small hope, and she clung to it desperately.

They were muffled, echoing. They were somewhere behind or above her. She couldn't get a sense of bearing, and she was almost positive a wall separated the voices from her. She heard a door swing open and the voices became clear. There was light, but she could barely see. Barely was still a distinct improvement and for now, she was willing to accept it.

"It's her. It's got to be," a young woman spoke. There was excitement and urgency in her voice.

"Josephine, really," something slid beneath Ren as the new woman spoke. She sounded more refined, though not much older. "She is the only one in here."

The voice named Josephine made a sound of refute. Without warning, Ren's vision returned, only to be blinded by a flashlight being shone into her eyes. She wanted to protest but nothing came.

"She's in there, but not by much yet," Josephine said to the other woman in the room. Her vision was now obscured by purple after images from the light but she could make out that the girl was looking elsewhere. "This might be a record."

"Her name is Florence Weatherbee." The other woman spoke again. Even paralyzed, Ren cringed inwardly. She wanted to tell them that she had buried that name. She hadn't been Florence in a long time.

Ren got the distinct impression that she was travelling again. As the after images faded, she took in the room. She couldn't move her eyes, but her peripheral vision was still intact. Her soul shuddered a little as her brain put all the pieces together. It only took a minute; she had seen enough television shows to know what a morgue looked like. She had been rescued from a drawer, and was now resting in a wheelchair. Her body did not seem to be cooperating as the young voice helped her into some ill-fitting clothes. It wasn't even that her body didn't cooperate; it didn't work at all. The other woman seemed more interested in other things as she stood at a desk, rifling through papers. What were they doing here?

As if reading her thoughts, the voice called Josephine held Ren's face in her hands, smiling.

"My name's Josephine. You can call me Joe if you like," A pair of sparkling golden eyes peered through a pointy mop of chestnut hair. Her nose wrinkled when she smiled and Ren thought for a moment she might smile back out of infectious reflex. Her head settled on her chest again, allowing her to watch Josephine fiddle with the buttons on a shirt that Ren had never seen before, but apparently was now wearing. Her legs were bare. A chill coursed through her: Had she been naked? What happened to her clothes?

Joe finished the buttons and straightened the hem on the shirt, trying to provide Ren a bit of decency. She nodded satisfactorily and smiled, holding Ren's face again in her hands as she made eye contact.

"This is a rescue mission. Trust me, you don't want to be here when the autopsy starts."

Autopsy? But that can't be! I'm not... am I?

But no one responded. All Ren could do was observe and hope her condition would improve.

"She's belted in," Josephine lurched the chair back and forth; Ren's head bobbing. The other woman did not stray from the desk. She appeared to be busy on the computer.

"Um, vroom vroom?" Josephine jostled the chair as she made the car sounds. Again, no response.

"Mariel —" She tried a third time and was interrupted by a curt and cool two-word response.

"Almost finished."

Josephine pushed the chair toward the door. Ren could still make out Mariel in her peripheral vision. She was intently focused; Ren could see that from the stern gaze and intolerant brow as she willed the computer to follow her commands.

In another world, Alternate Universe Ren was having the time of her life, falling in with a gang of rogue CIA ninjas. In that far away place, she was about to start a journeymanship into a world of hacking, espionage and covert awesomeness. But in this universe, Ren was trapped inside an unresponsive body with an all-too-friendly stranger amid a rescue she wasn't aware she needed. And she was quite possibly dead. Alternate Universe Ren was always the lucky one.

"Done." Mariel clicked a couple more times, shutting down the terminal and grabbing a manila folder from the desk. She strode quickly, kneeling in front of Ren, holding her face like Josephine had. Ren looked into a pair of steel blue eyes that scrutinized her, locking eyes with her in the same uncomfortable way her optometrist often did. It was as if they didn't believe the occupant was actually at home, so they were peeping in the windows to make sure. Layered blonde bangs swung back and forth as she regarded the unresponsive girl, her pink lips hardly noticeable in their thin, taut line.

Mariel's sharp gaze softened as she looked into Ren's face. For a brief moment, Mariel looked sad, lost. It dissipated and her controlled exterior returned with a slight upturn of the corners of her mouth. She almost looked warm, inviting, but Ren saw the look moments before and knew that this was a front to keep things moving. Mariel was a deeper well than she wanted to let on.

"Florence, my name is Mariel. You must be so confused right now. We can explain – but later. We are going now." She caressed Ren's face softly. "You are going to be fine, Florence. I need you to believe that."

Ren didn't bother to question why she took these strange women on faith. But she did believe Mariel. It was suddenly not a question: Mariel and Josephine were here to rescue her.

The trip through the hospital was uneventful, which Ren assumed was the best outcome. There had been a slight hiccup when they had to transfer Ren from the wheelchair to the car, but the parking lot was practically empty. It was dark. Ren assumed the middle of the night.

The streetlights had been hypnotic, the

conversation minimal. What she had gathered was from Josephine reading the file out loud. It was the accident report that had been delivered by the police along with Ren's body.

"You know, she's really lucky that she's not worse for wear. Listen to this: Victim was found 45 meters from point of impact. Evidence of collision apparent on vehicle: Damage to lower front windshield, denting above bumper on –"

"Josephine!"

"What?" She looked at Mariel, and then cast a thoughtless glance over her shoulder into the back seat where Ren was propped up on a corner, half gazing out the window, half staring at the interior roof. She had a full second to stare dumbfounded at Mariel again before shame descended on her. "Oh god –"

She was stammering out an apology, but Ren had already zoned out. Her mind was piecing together her last moments. She would have cried, flailed, leapt from the car to get away from these thoughts, but here, stuck, she had no choice but to let them flit together and confront her.

Her last moment played on a loop in her head. Each time, she tried to find one of the million options that might have been available to her in order to escape this fate. All empty possibilities, she knew, because she was still here. Mariel and Josephine were arguing in the front seat. Ren wondered if she could sleep in her condition, and if she could do it with her eyes open.

* * * *

She likened it less to sleeping and more to a fever dream. She found a space to stare off into that, mostly, gave her peace enough to drift somewhere else. The car ride was long. Dawn was breaking beyond the clouds by the time the car stopped. As Mariel and Josephine withdrew her from the car, something had changed. Ren was aware of being handled. Before, she knew it was happening because she could see it, hear it, but she never felt it. Were her senses returning? Excitedly, she tried to speak, move, wiggle her fingers, anything. She tried to pacify herself. Obviously it wasn't going to be like flipping a switch. She tried to blink, or move her eyes, something small, but nothing happened.

Yet. But something is happening.

As they carried her, she felt warmth. Not bodily warmth, but almost an energy that radiated from Josephine and Mariel. It spread through whatever energy she still possessed, fueling her hope and curiosity. It reminded her of the warm glow after the accident, but stronger.

Ren was placed in a chair, and Mariel resumed her position before the unresponsive girl. Her hair had been tied back earlier; it was now hanging in long waves of platinum and gold around her shoulders. They shared a gaze and behind Mariel's eyes, again Ren saw something: another flash of sadness that could not be put into words. She wondered if there was an explanation for it, if anyone knew. She wanted to ask, but that would have to wait. Mariel brought her walls up again, resuming her refined exterior and smiled softly as she held the girl's face in her hands.

"You feel trapped in there, I know." Ren felt the warmth reaching her again as Mariel spoke. She could feel it in her shoulder as well and wondered if Josephine was beside her, lurking outside her vision.

"It may sound preposterous, but the best thing for you right now is to stay calm. You are going to be fine." She wanted to nod, to communicate that she *was* fine and she could already feel herself getting better. Mariel looked down and took her hand, and Ren knew that the veil was drawn again. Something about all this troubled Mariel and Ren had the distinct feeling that it wasn't just about her.

"Florence, there is no easy way to say this next part, unbelievable as it is," She looked up, a tear trailing down her cheek. "You died."

In the hours since their daring rescue, Ren had already exhausted the limited possibilities. But to hear it from someone so visibly moved finally made it real for her. A wave crashed down around her brain, flooding her thoughts with all the ifs and coulds, wills and can'ts this new realization provided. She wanted – no, she *needed* – to communicate now. She had questions that would not wait.

"We brought you here so you could be among people who know what you are. Do you understand? You are not alone in this." Mariel swallowed and looked away.

Josephine joined Mariel in front of the chair; she pulled Mariel's head onto her own shoulder and whispered softly, something Ren couldn't make out. She then knotted her fingers with the other two hands, making a gnarled ball of fists. She tried to smile and now Ren knew something was going on. It was not the same infectious smile that she had seen earlier. This was forced – like Mariel's – for some yet unknown reason.

"This isn't easy to say, but we're sisters now," Josephine tried to smile, putting off the inevitable. Her eyes widened as she realized how the words might be interpreted. "That's not the bad news – at least I hope not. The bad news is that even though you're fine here, to the rest of the world you are dead. That includes your friends and family." Ren felt her heart sink to somewhere around the pit of her stomach. "It's best to let them grieve and move on, trust me." Ren watched her blink away a tear and saw that same sadness inside Josephine.

Was this her future? A brand new life full of sadness and solitude? No, she wouldn't have it. She would carve the life she wanted, no matter what. She would miss her friends, but a distance had been yawning open between them for a while. In the three years since her mother died, she'd had good days and bad; mostly bad. Her friends did what they could, but they had no basis for her struggle, so when she had a bad day, they were nowhere to be found. In the beginning, she'd hardly noticed. It was easy to retreat beneath the blankets and simply call the day a loss. But as she tried to return to the world, as she forced herself to seek out the company of people who might be able to show her how to be a functioning human again, that was where she noticed the problems surfacing. They could take her out and show her a good time, but they could no longer provide anything more than small talk. They didn't want to discuss anything deep enough to upset her – and they weren't sure what might upset her, so they just didn't talk about anything. Her friends became superficial to the point of being unnecessary, so she decided she was simply better off.

Her mother, on the other hand, was everywhere. The longer Ren lived without her, the more things seemed to appear to remind her of all the wonderful things her mother had shared. Ren had continued to put aside money here and there between rent and college loans, still planning on taking that backpacking trip through Europe that her mother convinced her to do. In the meantime, she spent most of her days picking up her mother's hobbies: reading in the warm afternoon sun, maintaining a small garden on her windowsill, living day to day as if tomorrow would never come. Often, she had to battle herself to be responsible enough to keep a roof over her head, which made her smile. It was the way her mother lived. It was also why mom got the hippie funeral of her dreams – she had never bothered to think far enough into the future to plan for the end. It was up to Ren to call around to the remaining family and scrounge enough money to pay for a plot and a priest.

And even though she had found his number, she never bothered to call her father. She might have been able to guilt him into paying the expenses, maybe even helping her with the rest of the affairs, but she just couldn't bring herself to do that. He left when she was only six. It had been in the middle of the night and in the middle of an argument. Her mother always changed the subject when asked what had happened, so Ren stopped asking. Even if he'd regretted his choice, he'd never made it known to her and had never bothered to find her; she had decided he wasn't worth the trouble at all.

She felt pressure on her hand and realized that Josephine was holding it tight. She had drifted off. Those golden eyes drifted back to her focus and she realized that the girl had stopped to collect herself.

"We've both been there. All of us have, actually. You're going to get through this too. We'll be with you every step of the way." Josephine half-smiled through wet eyes.

Ren hated her body more now than any moment of glaring self-conscious behavior had ever made her. She needed her voice to protest, her hands to throw themselves around in frustration, her legs to stride her out of this room in a huff. But mostly, she needed to scream uncontrollably, and to cry. She needed to cry for this loss of self, for all the confusion, for the things that had and had not happened in her life, and for all the things that might not happen now. She wanted to punch something. She had never done that before: hauled off and punched something out of frustration. It had always seemed so barbaric, but now she realized that she simply had no point of reference before.

Yes, she wanted to scream until she shook, to punch until things hurt, to rage until she collapsed.

But nothing moved, nothing raged. Not a single part of her responded to her bidding. Only her own thoughts rattling around in her brain, and the certainty that they would slowly drive her insane.

Josephine looked up and smiled, brushing away one hot tear as it rolled down Ren's cheek.

"That's it, girl. You'll be back with us in no time."

As if to cue the bittersweet triumph of the moment, violins sang sweetly in the background. Lost to the moment and her thoughts, Ren had never noticed Mariel slip away. Josephine rolled her eyes and held up a finger, leaving Ren to her place in the chair, where she could mostly see the exchange about to take place.

"Oh no. You did that to me, I'm not going to let you do that to her too."

"What are you talking about?"

"This. Brahms. No way."

"She needs something soothing right now, Josephine."

"But Brahms isn't soothing to everyone. Mostly just to you."

Mariel crossed her arms, her mouth pursed and she looked like she had been slighted. The waves of her hair shook as if they too were offended by Joe's opinion.

"And you are suddenly the resident expert on all things Florence Weatherbee?"

She could only see Josephine's back but imagined that she was sticking her tongue out at Mariel.

"I'm observant."

Mariel looked between the two girls, as if they had been conspiring behind her back, then stepped aside with a flourishing gesture.

"By all means."

She saw Josephine click away at a keyboard and realized that if she could, she would be smiling. It was starting to sink in that they might be telling her the truth. She might be sitting here, dead or dying or vice versa, in a room with a couple of complete strangers, but she wasn't alone. And against all odds, they did truly seem to care about her. It was a small comfort in the world of weirdness she found herself swimming in.

All things considered, she didn't have any of the heavy thoughts and creeping fears that dying people usually contended with. If she was already dead, there was no worry about dying. No worries about if there was an after, because there was — for her, anyway. For Ren, death wasn't scary at all. Maybe it was because her death had brought her a new family, or because her death wasn't much of a death at all.

Maybe it was because Josephine had, whether by plan or accident, decided on Dead Can Dance and — oh, how Ren wished she could dance right now. Was it the speakers or her new perspective that made the melody sound so rich and inviting? She didn't care. She wanted to close her eyes and fully immerse herself in the music, in the moment. She promised to give Josephine a hug as soon as she was able. She had missed the end of the exchange between Mariel and Josephine, but it sounded as if Mariel had conceded.

Josephine returned, holding her hand.

"I really hope this is tolerable," she lowered her voice and gestured toward Mariel with her eyes. "Because Brahms, right?" There was another huff from Mariel, whose hearing seemed to be exceptional. "We're going to give you some peace and quiet now, let you rest."

Mariel had returned as well, none of the former bickering present.

"Try to relax. I know it is not easy, but your thoughts will drive you crazy after a while." She smiled as if from experience. "We will see progress before you know it."

It was a lingering moment, and Ren almost expected them to keep talking. Or maybe kiss her goodnight. Something. They dimmed the lights as they left the room, the music continuing to churn around her, the melodies swirling, pulling her along, away from her thoughts for a while. She smiled inwardly; Mariel sounded pretty confident. What it all meant, she wasn't quite sure, but she assumed it meant that she might be back on her feet before long.

TWO

"Dammit Joe, I don't want to!"

"Ren, stop being such a baby! Get out of the chair and walk!"

"No!"

"Do it!"

"You can't make me!"

"Want to see me try?"

"No. I am tired of these lessons. I give up!"

Three months ago, throwing up her hands in frustration was a dream. Now she did it daily, sometimes more than once. She was still a long way from storming out of the room in a huff, however. She couldn't even shuffle out of the room, huff or no. Josephine did her best to keep

Ren moving forward in her recovery, but three months of the same sights and the same routine had made her stir crazy. So had Mariel's strange sense of rewarding progress: until she could walk again, she was confined to the common rooms on the first floor. She understood that it was mostly for her own safety and benefit, but having a place to storm off to would have been nice on occasion.

Slowly, over the last three months, she had reclaimed every one of her natural abilities. Her sight and hearing seemed to come first, as well as her other sensory nerves. Her involuntary functions followed. She had grown so accustomed to being without a heartbeat that when it began again, she was terrified. Ducts and glands and organs all began full-scale production once again, although as Joe pointed out, they had actually never ceased to function except at the time of her death. Her heart was moving so slowly in the beginning that it wouldn't register, even on the best machines. Her lungs were acting on a similar set of directions, only giving her what she needed at the time as the rest of her body rebooted. Fortunately, when none of your functions are actually functioning, there isn't a lot of need for oxygen. It was mostly there to keep her brain going, which had only been down long enough to reboot.

Josephine did what she could in the way of basic tutoring. She had been through the same process and remembered a lot of the questions she had asked herself amidst recovery. There were no in-depth explanations, but she was able to provide a pretty solid set of answers for the questions Ren was unable to ask yet.

"Yes, it was a real death. No, it doesn't make us zombies or vampires or any other supernatural creature. Yes, it is still technically supernatural. No, we don't know of anything else like us. We stop aging at the time of death, and continue on from there. We never grow any older, no matter how many years pass. No, no one has been dumb enough to test whether or not we'd come back again. Don't give it another thought."

When the small muscle functions returned, Ren was so disappointed she couldn't cry out. She spent a full day just enjoying the luxury of closing her eyes on her own. She enjoyed her first night of peaceful sleep that same evening. And then it occurred to her that her eyes could help her communicate as well. Fortunately, Joe seemed to understand. She could communicate in yes and no answers with the movement of her eyes. It wasn't speaking yet, but it was something.

Slowly, her small muscles recovered, and then bigger systems began to wake up. She found that she could wiggle her toes and fingers, and then her arms and legs. Eventually, all the little groups that worked together to create her voice got together and the struggle to learn to talk began.

The problem was not that her muscles didn't function, they would return to her, without any atrophy, even. The problem was being able to do something with the finesse of a fully functioning human being. She could lift objects in her hands without a problem. It took time and patience to be able to hold a glass of water and drink from it without spilling the whole thing all over herself. Soup wasn't even a consideration for the first few months. Likewise, she could make noises all she wanted, and she knew the words, but being able to force those sounds to become words took time.

She worked at it, and she worked hard. She

was able to wheel herself all around the ground floor in her chair. She could prepare meals and get around like a champion, but her legs frustrated her beyond belief. She could not force them to cooperate with her, not like the other muscles in her body. There were too many things that she had no conscious control over, and the longer she failed to make it work, the more unbearable she became around the others.

Mariel had surrendered to Ren's frustrating tantrums early on, only checking in when she was certain that Ren was in a good mood, or utterly defeated by the day's struggles. Joe, on the other hand, welcomed a challenge and happily volunteered to participate in Ren's recovery. She enjoyed having someone to butt heads with.

"If you can walk out of this room, I will surrender." She gestured to the door. "After you, mademoiselle."

"Oh, sure. Pick on the girl in the wheelchair." She locked the wheels and braced herself on the arms of the chair.

Joe laughed. "You're only in a wheelchair because you refuse to get off your lazy butt." She crossed to Ren's side, ready to help if she was needed. "Which I believe is getting bigger, thanks to all your sitting around."

"Shut up." Ren groaned and pushed herself up on her arms, trying to get her feet under her. She hated this part. Sometimes her legs cooperated; sometimes an impulse would cause her to wind up in a heap on the floor. Whether Josephine understood or not, it was embarrassing. Ren wasn't terribly athletic in her former life, but she was no slouch. She had a gift for walking. Boots, heels, or flip-flops, she could walk in anything through anything, and never get tripped up. Now she was having trouble keeping her bare feet beneath her.

You get hit by one bus and everything changes.

Mariel had explained what she could, in as plain of terms as she was able. Her answers weren't much beyond Joe's, unfortunately. Resurrection wasn't an exact science. Death was like a blackout to the physical body. Everything but the brain went through a hard reset and needed retraining from square one. It was all a matter of telling the brain where all the pathways connected, which no one could consciously do, unfortunately. Manual dexterity tests made Ren want to throw things. Ironically, she needed the dexterity she couldn't master to throw anything hard enough to feel vindicated. With Joe's insistence, she re-mastered abilities that she had once dominated as a child. Even meeting with success time and again, Ren was reaching a boiling point easier and more often.

Mariel greeted instructor and student at the end of each lesson with tea. Ren pointed out that she didn't like tea, but Mariel insisted. At least it wasn't being served to her in a sippy cup anymore.

"The tea itself is not important," Mariel smiled softly. "What matters is that we can take ten minutes out of the day to sit calmly and enjoy the company of our sisters – regardless of how we feel about our day and our routine."

Ren knew what she meant. These were the people she was going to start her new life with; she could be a little nicer. She didn't want to be nicer, though. She wanted Joe to suffer with her, to feel her anguish as she felt it. The whole experience had formed a hard shell around her heart, and though the logical part of her brain told her otherwise, her emotional center didn't think that her housemates truly appreciated the hardship she'd gone through.

"Well, the routine blows too," she hadn't meant to say it out loud. There was time to take it back, to apologize, but she didn't. She let the words hang in the air until Joe stood up.

"On that note, maybe we should give you some alone time and –"

"No, Josephine. I do not think she has finished." Mariel turned to Ren. The refined exterior usually operated as a wall to shield something soft and fragile inside. Ren could see it in her eyes that wasn't the case today.

"No, it's fine." Ren spoke the words into the room, but the room knew she didn't mean them.

Mariel set her cup down on the table, folding her hands across her lap. "Please, speak your mind. It is obvious there is something you need to get off your chest."

"I don't think you understand how hard this is," she slapped the arms of her chair, wanting to emphasize the point she was trying to get across.

Joe hid her face in her hands, peeking through her fingers as if she was watching a scary movie.

"Ren, you should –"

"Hush, Josephine. Let her speak."

Ren continued to flail looking back and forth at the two women, one passive and the other dismayed.

"I am exhausted. Every molecule in me is bruised and all you can say is 'Good job, Ren!', 'Keep going, Ren!', 'Let's have tea, Ren!' You're not helping."

Mariel didn't move. Her face was still, unreadable. Then, slowly, she blinked and stood up. She turned and walked toward the study. She did not turn when she spoke.

"You can be excused from tea time then. I apologize that we are not assisting your recovery."

Ren watched the door close. It occurred to her that she had won the argument, but it didn't feel like a victory. All the frustration that had been building up simply deflated, leaving her empty. She turned to Joe and her breath caught.

Joe was still holding her face, but it wasn't in fear, it was sadness. Tears were streaming from her eyes and she cupped her mouth to silence the sounds.

"Joe, I —" She wanted to tell Joe that she didn't understand what was going on. Joe stood quickly, turning the wheel chair violently and pushing Ren into the guest room she'd been staying in. Ren tried to speak again, but Joe whirled the chair, catching Ren by surprise. When Ren looked up, she met a wide and burning gaze. Joe mashed the spacebar on the computer and then pressed hard on the volume button. It didn't matter what played, Joe needed something to cover up the noise.

"Mariel is almost 200 years old," Joe spoke as evenly as she could. Her voice had a consistent quiver to it, as she ignored the tears streaming down her face. "She did not get this far because she is a thoughtless, inconsiderate woman."

"I didn't mean —"

"She rescued you without a thought for her own safety. We could have been arrested — and that would mean being discovered. She took you in and has been nothing but kind to you."

"Joe, I'm sorry." It was all she could say. The weight of her mistake had started pressing on her as soon as she got mouthy with Mariel. The longer Joe spoke, the worse she felt.

"No. That's not going to cut it. I'm not who you need to apologize to." Joe backed away from Ren, retreating to the wall where she sank to the floor. "You have no idea what kind of hell she has been through – what she goes through every time she finds one of us. It's like re-opening her own house of horrors."

Joe wiped at her face, smearing mascara and tears.

"She was the first; she didn't get rescued."

Ren shook her head. She didn't understand what Joe was talking about. The words echoed in her brain, rebounding and sharpening themselves against her wits until it was clear that she would never unlearn the meaning. The regret hiding in the pit of her stomach was now a crushing pain in her heart as the understanding took hold and she realized how childish and selfish she was, how terrible she'd been to both of them.

"Mariel doesn't talk about it, and no one knows how long she was buried." Joe glared at Ren, to be certain she wouldn't make another false step when speaking to Mariel. "She had to relearn the basics wrapped in a death shroud, under six feet of dirt, inside a coffin. She saved you from a hell you can't even fathom."

The hard shell around Ren's heart dissolved in the sadness that flooded her. She felt cold pouring out into her extremities, emanating from a hole in her soul. She felt like a monster; a bitter, selfish monster. No amount of apologizing was going to fix this, but she had to start somewhere. She would not let the silence linger a second time today.

Joe sniffled, wiping her eyes and nose on her shirtsleeve. She looked up and saw Ren locking her wheels and then gripping the arms of the chair as if she meant to stand.

"Let it go, Ren, training isn't going to help anything now."

Ren gritted her teeth, focusing on the door.

"I'm not training," she took a breath, puffing it out. "I need to go apologize."

Her arms quaked as she pushed herself up. Her leg muscles felt tiny, useless, as she tried to move her legs underneath her for support. She fell back in the chair, growled, and started again.

"Ren, stop."

"No," Now it was Ren's turn to look crazed with a face full of hot tears. "You're right. She has been wonderful, and I was a brat. I can't leave it like that." She ignored the screaming in her muscles, begging her to stop and pushed herself up on wobbly legs, holding tight to the chair and the wall for support. Joe was on her feet too, watching.

"Then get back in the chair and you can apologize."

Ren stared at her. Joe nodded and opened the door.

Each step was followed by minutes of balance corrections and grunting as she tried to get the next step under way. Training had set her in the right direction; she could feel it. Her body knew how it was supposed to work; it just wasn't supplying enough power to the right places yet.

It took her ten minutes to get out of the room and into the common area. Once there, everything got harder. There were no walls, nothing to support her until she reached the couches in the middle of the room. She could get two paces, on the rare occasion three, before collapsing hard on her knees. Then she had to find a way to stand back up before she could continue her slow shamble across to the study.

All this effort, Ren calculated, was less of a struggle than finding the right words to form her apology. She had apologized for stupid things before, but nothing this monumental. No level of self-absorbed idiocy could rival this. This was the biggest mistake she had made in her life, hands down. She took every bit of the pain she was suffering on her trek across the room as part of her retribution, uncertain it would ever be enough.

The further she went, her already weak muscles began to quake and buckle. It was taking longer to get back on her feet after every collapse, and she was barely making two steps any more. She was barely halfway across the room, falling forward again when the study door opened.

Mariel took one look and didn't hesitate. She went directly to Ren's side to comfort her.

"You should not be away from the chair till you are ready."

"I needed to make amends."

"No, you do not. I understand."

"No, *I* understand. Joe —" The air between them changed. She felt Mariel stiffen. Ren's tears revisited her. "She told me. I know there is nothing I can say to make up for it."

"You were unaware."

"That's not an excuse."

Mariel nodded, she was still silent, reserved. Ren put her arms around her to pull her close.

"I am so sorry," Ren spoke quietly, her voice strained. "For everything you've been through. For everything I will never go through, because of you."

Mariel hugged her back, the words meaning more than Ren could have expected.

"And I will drink any tea you set before me, I promise."

Mariel laughed through half-sobs.

"I am certain we can find something you enjoy. It defeats the purpose if you are not enjoying it."

"Speaking of which," Joe chimed in as she carried a tray with fresh cups – and a box of tissues – from the kitchen. She set the tray on the coffee table and returned to pull Ren off the floor and help her to the couch.

Mariel and Ren sat beside one another while Joe poured the cups. She passed a box of assorted tea packets to Ren, who decided trial by fire was best, grabbing the first she could in shaky hands. Joe assisted with the tea, and Ren took her time, wondering if maybe she shouldn't request a sippy cup just one last time.

They enjoyed their tea in relative silence, and Ren realized that tea, at least this variety, wasn't so bad. She would never fully succumb, though. She loved her coffee far too much.

After a second cup for each of them, Mariel broke the silence by setting her teacup on the table and standing up. "I will see the two of you in a couple hours," She waved a finger and smiled. "Try to stay friendly."

Ren raised an eyebrow. "Where are you off to?"

"Colette should be at the airport shortly. Someone should be there to greet her."

"Colette?"

Mariel raised an eyebrow, suppressing a smirk. "You didn't think it was just the three of us, did you?"

"Well, I guess I..." Ren didn't know how to finish the sentence. She didn't know what she thought. Everything she thought she knew was a tiny speck in a rapidly expanding universe, but if she was lucky, she would have plenty of time to consider that expanding unknown. "Two hundred years…"

"Give or take," Mariel winked.

* * * *

Two more weeks of Joe's continued abuse and Ren was finally rewarded for her efforts with a tour of the upper floors. In her dreams, she imagined it as a musical montage; complete with chandeliers, singing servants and many, many open-armed twirls through large ballrooms. The truth was far less gratifying. In all the muscles that had been reconditioned for living, it was apparent that none of them were the muscles used to climb stairs. These still felt very underdeveloped, making the first flight of stairs a painful preview of the rest of the tour.

Still, Ren was not one to back down from a challenge. The tour must go on… regardless how long it would take.

Three full stories of bedrooms, workrooms, and storage, most of which Mariel declared as "at your disposal." She was shown to a corner room, empty and unadorned, except for a bed and dresser. Ren walked inside, leaning against the sill, her face almost pressed against the glass. The windows gave her a pleasant view of the oversized lawn bordered by streetlights that wandered off into the dark down the row.

"I thought you might like this room," Mariel spoke quietly from the doorway. "It was mine once, long ago."

Ren turned back, trying to smile appreciatively, playing with the buttons on the shirt she was wearing, one of many borrowed items she'd been wearing since her arrival.

"Yes, those too," she laughed. "Live long enough and everything becomes hand-me-downs for other people." Ren smiled, looking around the room. She was caught between the sensation of emptiness the room reflected on her own consciousness, and the potential for renewal. The room needed a fresh coat of paint and some new adornments. Ren realized her own life was about ready for the same thing.

It sounded petty, but she missed her clothes. She missed flowing fabrics with tails and hanging accents left for the wind to play with. She missed the feel of the wind, the sensation of flying, or the appearance of it. Being pronounced dead probably meant that her apartment had been emptied. She hoped some nice people owned her belongings now.

She sat on the edge of the bed and let the shock sink in: as far as the rest of the world was concerned, she really was dead, and had been for about half a year. Her thoughts drifted to her friends, and she tried to shut them out. Yes, they had drifted apart, but two things always brought people together: weddings and funerals. She didn't want to think about her friends wondering, regretting. She cut herself off; she couldn't do it. The idea of them gathering to mourn her, she couldn't think of that; it would tear her apart. She squeezed her eyes shut and tried to think of something else. Anything else. She sniffled a little and wiped at her eyes. It was almost unbelievable after everything else that she had experienced that she still had tears left inside her.

"It gets easier with time," Mariel slowly walked into the room. She moved to the window, looking out at the city lights. She paused, putting a hand on the sill before turning to Ren. "There will be days when you forget you are not human anymore. You might even fall in love."

Ren tried to suppress a gasp. She was on the verge of tears over absent friends and a missing wardrobe; love was a long way from where she was sitting.

"You will find that you can do most of the things you did before; more really. Mortality has a way of making us cautious. Do not be fooled though, you can still bleed, and break bones. The pain will still be there. Take risks, but not unnecessary ones."

Ren looked up at her, trying to smile. "You make it sound so like such a good life."

Mariel sat down next to her, putting a hand in hers. "We have been given a second chance; cherish this one while we have it."

Mariel squeezed her hand again. The look in her eyes told Ren everything she needed to know. It was a good life; certainly better than not having one at all. She nodded and looked around the room again at the bare walls, the empty closet.

"Don't you worry your pretty little head about this sad state of affairs," Josephine came into the room, spinning like a fairy godmother. "Tomorrow is going to be an amazing day."

She broke the melancholy spell of the room as she pulled Ren from her seat, forcing her to turn.

"Okay, what is so special about tomorrow?"

Joe smiled like the sun. "Tomorrow, we shop! No more plain-Jane – er, Ren. Some threads, some paint, maybe a mirror ball..."

Ren's eyes widened, caught between the dream of making her sad little room a comfortable existence and lacking a way to pay for it all. Joe knew the look, and shook her.

"You don't have to worry – it's covered."

"How?"

Joe directed her attention to Mariel. Ren followed the gaze.

"The paperwork is already started. Colette is working out the details. Relax; it's not some devil's deal. We all earn our keep and in return, we get to lead a comfortable existence. As soon as you are comfortable, we will start showing you the rest of the ropes."

Ren just blinked. The gears were no longer turning; too much new at one time brought the gears to a grinding halt. Mariel put a hand to Ren's cheek, smiling before she left the room.

"It will be fine, Ren. You are a Delaney now."

* * * *

Ren watched the scenery outside the windows turn from their lush quiet neighborhood to busy streets of bustling Marysville as Mariel's sedan moved slowly along the city streets. Joe pointed out landmarks and local shops that they could explore sometime. They had left the slow pace of the residential neighborhood behind them. These streets were wide and full of cars rushing in all directions. Beyond the immediate street, where shops and restaurants flew past their windows, tall buildings stood proud in the background, dominating the skyline. There were only a handful of towers to speak of, and not truly a skyscraper-dominated metropolis, but Ren knew from the sight of them that she had been promoted to big city life and would have to learn to deal with that – if she ever bothered leaving the house again. Traffic did not appear to be very hospitable from her vantage point in the back seat. In the front seats, Mariel drove while Colette quietly cursed the other drivers on the road.

"I'm almost certain our insurance will forgive us for a single accident."

Ren swallowed, not sure she wanted to be in a car with someone encouraging an accident.

"I will not hit someone if it can be avoided."

Colette cursed again as Mariel was forced to brake hard, the two girls in the back yelping as they lurched in their seats.

"I'm just pointing out that we are in pretty favorable standing, in case someone needs to be taught a lesson."

To Colette's disappointment, they arrived at their destination unscathed. Ren rubbed at her belly and her shoulder where the seatbelt had cut in, certain there would be a bruise before the day's end. Joe pulled Ren from her thoughts both figuratively and literally, taking her hands and twirling her before throwing up her arms in a grandiose gesture.

"May I present the Marysville Mall," she paused, scowling when the expected applause did not arrive. "One hundred fourteen restaurants, department stores and boutiques to capture your very imagination!"

"If your imagination can only be captured on a bank statement," Colette droned, but winked at Ren. They had not had much of an opportunity to get to know one another, but Ren thought she liked Colette well enough. She wore glasses even though Ren suspected they were not necessary, but the tortoise shell frames accented her brown eyes so well, it was hard to argue. Her hair was always wrapped up in a twist or a knot, sealing that air of professionalism that her wardrobe already conveyed.

She looked up at Ren, smiling. "Don't worry about the money. Have fun today."

Ren didn't keep the fun to herself in the least. It's a little known fact that money can in fact buy happiness – at the right times and in the right doses. As four women went store to store, laughing and carrying on and helping one of their own find a part of herself she'd lost, they found the perfect combination that made a perfect day of consumer therapy.

They'd debated Ren's fashion choices with

her, imparted some ideas of their own, and in general found her a little bit of everything she might need for the next year or more. By the end of the day, they were all overloaded with bags, forming a wagon train to protect themselves from the mall rats as they took in a late lunch at the food court.

"I really hope you have everything you need for a while," Colette looked across the table as she massaged her wrists, creased and red with lines where the shopping bags had cut in.

She pulled at a cheese stick, cutting the stretching fibers with her teeth and smiled. "I really don't know how to thank you enough for doing this. It's…" she started to choke up a little.

Joe put her arm around Ren's shoulders as Mariel reached out across the table. "They might only be things, but they help you feel more like you. It's thanks enough."

Colette cleared her throat. "Usually Mariel is the one who reminds us when we are bringing a bit too much attention to ourselves, but I should probably point out that having a good group cry in the middle of the food court is a bit conspicuous."

Immediately, the tears dried up on cheeks red with embarrassment and laughter.

THREE

Ren had often imagined what immortality might be like. She imagined epic tales, quests, kingdoms and most likely a dragon or two for slaying. She assumed that immortality was reserved for only the greatest of champions and bravest of heroes. A life of obscurity, hidden behind a secret identity... and maybe a fancy lair built around that secret identity.

Somehow, an eternity spent caretaking over early American history on the outskirts of frantic, populated Marysville seemed more like a punishment than a reward. Perhaps she wasn't as righteous as her 'bravest of heroes', but she certainly wasn't wicked enough to have this thrust upon her.

Maybe you should read the fine print next time you make a deal with the devil.

Except that there was no fine print. No contract. There was no offer to speak of. She was being given a do-over, and she didn't even have to risk her soul. At least not that she was aware.

Colette had explained that many years ago, she and Mariel set up a grant for the house. Originally, it was to proclaim the house as a historical monument, so that it couldn't be torn down or sold off by the city. Then, they created a foundation that "maintained" the house and started working toward turning it into a museum.

While the museum was in fact a front, it served a purpose as well. It gave Mariel a chance to share intimate history with further generations. Facts and items that might have been overlooked by historians were all carefully audited and collected in the house while she, Colette and a few of the earliest additions settled in under the first roof they shared as a family. The same roof she and William shared when they tried starting a family of their own. Everything she did after that was to carry on William's legacy, to keep his memory alive.

Once they set the plan in action, Colette began creating a cycle of "volunteers" that managed the house's front rooms, the proper museum. As more girls appeared, they found it easier to cycle the "volunteers" every couple of years. While none of the girls ever bothered to change their names, or keep up appearances, the paperwork was immaculate – and always just a little behind. Mariel had decided that Delaney House would be neither the rule nor the exception. She wanted to keep off the radar completely. The truth, as they would learn, was that no one actually cared. No one bothered to make sure that Delaney House was running proper books, or was putting their grant funds to good use. But they kept up appearances to make certain their secret would be safe. The grant money was enough to keep up appearances, but they existed off Mariel's fortune of rare antiquities and Colette's wise investments.

If it weren't for appearances, Ren would be out of a job completely. Traffic through the museum, even though open, was sparse and predictable. Friday mornings, Saturday afternoons, and event days brought in traffic, but little else. She spent most days memorizing details; not always by choice, but sometimes there was not much else to do without visitors.

The house was, oddly enough, the perfect place for Ren and her newfound sisters to hide in plain sight, although 'house' was a misnomer. The house was a nine-bedroom mansion complete with a library, two parlor rooms, a primary and secondary kitchen, four bathrooms, and the great common room that functioned as living, dining and ballroom – though it had not seen an actual ball in many years. It had been expanded over several renovations, each orchestrated by Mariel herself, but the original house was designed and built by its namesake: William Delaney.

"General William Delaney, commander in the United States Army, might have been one of the greatest strategic minds the Civil War had ever known," she paused her recitation, trying to remember what she had written in her notes. "Except General Delaney died days before the beginning of the Civil War."

She studied her reflection, looking at her note

cards again as she straightened her shirt. Her fingers fumbled with the tie again, only seeming to create a fisherman's loop around her neck. She smiled, unable to suppress a laugh. Mariel insisted on an upscale dress code while tending to the museum and its patrons. For Ren, it felt a little like a Catholic school uniform, and the house did have a boarding school feel, but Mariel never tried to interfere with Ren's dark makeup or her deep purple hair. She had been wrestling lately with the desire to change the color, as often happened, but she found it was one of the last ties to 'old Ren', and she wasn't ready to let go of that anchor just yet, so the purple stayed.

She turned away from the mirror, closing her eyes and imagining herself standing in the greeting room. She stood next to the fireplace, a larger than life painting of General Delaney hanging over the mantle. She took a breath, calling the words to her. William commanded respect and awe, in life and after. Ren aspired for even a modicum of that presence.

"After falling ill, he was shipped home, where the sickness became fever. He was quarantined and cared for by his wife alone." She paused again, always tripping over the meaning in those words. House arrest sounded almost romantic, if not for the fear of dying from some terrible virus.

"Fortunately, the fever did not pass beyond the walls of the house. Unfortunately, it claimed the lives of General Delaney and his young bride." She took a breath, suppressing a shudder. She remembered what Joe had told her about Mariel. She didn't want to think about it, yet couldn't stop herself.

"It is best not to dwell," Mariel stood in the doorway. It appeared by the look on her face that not only had she been listening, but she had been thinking about it too.

Ren folded her arms self-consciously. "I don't mean to, it's just..." Words rolled over her brain in a tidal pattern, in and out. She wanted to ask so many things, but the words continued to crash against a breaker. It told her that she knew better; now wasn't the time. "Does it get confusing? Keeping the history from the, um –"

"The truth?" Their eyes met, and Ren almost flinched. She hadn't meant to infer that they were lying.

Mariel walked into the room, gesturing for

the girl to come close. Her fingers expertly loosened the chaos around Ren's neck and convinced the fabric to bend to her will.

"It is not that hard to keep separate. One life ended, and a new one took its place." She gave a gentle tug, pushing the knot to its resting place under Ren's collar. "As far as anyone knows, we are a simple society intent on preserving William's memory. Which we are."

Ren turned back to the mirror, as if to examine Mariel's handiwork. They made eye contact in the reflection.

"There is no need to separate the two, Ren, but there is no reason to tell them everything either."

Mariel turned, leaving Ren to her thoughts. Her eyes returned to the notecards. Her fingers turned them, but her thoughts were elsewhere.

* * * *

Between Ren's introduction and Colette's return, the house managed to find an easy nice ebb and flow. Ren reasoned it was Colette's ability to balance herself between the factions that seemed to naturally occur: the stable against the reckless, the young against the established, the impulsive against the reserved. Colette stood between them all, the Great Negotiator. Normally, her presence was enough. Young enough to still enjoy a laugh with her sisters, but wise enough to understand that order and rules are what kept the house in one piece.

To keep their lives from being discovered, the sisters migrated between three houses. East, West and Central – where Delaney House resided – were available to each of them. Colette and Mariel regulated transfers to keep the general public from becoming suspicious. Though they tried to keep a rotation, it was not uncommon for some sisters to travel together.

Ren boggled at the idea that there were not only four of them, but an even dozen, spread out at different points. She wanted to know them all, to drive them crazy with interrogations, to know each and every detail. She had to continually remind herself that there was plenty of time to do so.

"Before long, the two of you are going to have to decide where you want to go next,"

Colette looked between the Ren and Joe. They looked at each other and instinctively took one another's hand.

Delaney House was a beacon for all sisters, a lighthouse in any storm. Ren smiled a little at each mention of 'sisters', as if they were a misfit pack of nuns. But they were definitely a sisterhood; there was no mistaking it. Each of them had a life after death to contend with, a new identity to replace the one stripped from them, a brand new life in a strange new world. They needed each other. Someone to comfort them when they woke up screaming, afraid they'd been buried alive. Someone to hold them and keep them strong when they longed for their old lives. The transition wasn't easy, but between them, they seemed to get through.

Ren hadn't reached any dark moments yet, and she hoped she wouldn't.

* * * *

Between her job, her passion, and her lack of answers, Ren found herself reading, researching and assaulting her sisters with questions constantly. She would not let rest that there were simply no answers to some questions. She resolved to leave 'why' for later. Someday, she would know why – why they came back, why them, and all of the why's that gnawed at her.

Colette and Joe had explained that second lives didn't seem to come very often, but when they did, each of the girls were aware.

"In my case, I was weak and starving to death," Colette shuddered, pushing the memory away. "The call came earlier, whenever my body decided it was really over. But we all feel it when there's a new one. Here, close your eyes."

Ren eyed her as Colette leaned across the table. She was expecting a prank. Colette straightened Ren's arms palm down.

"Really, close them." Colette insisted. Ren conceded, shutting her eyes.

"No peeking," Joe chided.

"Stop distracting her. Take a deep breath, Ren."

In the darkness behind her eyes, she waited. She inhaled deeply, feeling her chest expand. Slowly, she exhaled and drummed the pads of her fingers.

"Again." Colette spoke softly.

She breathed in again, pressing her palms flat. She paused before exhaling, cocking her head as if to listen for something. Instantly, she knew that she was using the wrong sense, but she didn't know what she was sensing, or what she was feeling it with.

"Breathe, Ren," Colette insisted. "And then tell me what you're feeling."

What am I feeling?

She couldn't find the words. At first, she was certain it was a sound, a vibration in the air. But she realized that she wasn't hearing anything. She thought perhaps a frequency of some sort, but then she could see it shimmering. No, not see. *Feel.*

Her face scrunched up as she tried to pin down the sensation and what it meant. She stilled. Before, it was everywhere, filling the room and all of her senses. Now, the sensation focused itself in a space just in front of her. She could almost see it; the way memories replayed themselves just behind her eyes. Immediately, it reminded her of the sensations she felt that first night that Joe and Mariel had come to her.

"It's a signal, and it's always there. It's a part of all of us," Joe explained, almost knowing the understanding as it played across Ren's face.

"If you learn to concentrate, you'll be able to tell where any of us are, anytime." Colette spoke, but it was almost background noise as she felt the glow brighten.

She reached out, wanting to grasp it. At first, she wasn't certain what she had laid hands on, but it wasn't a ball of light. It radiated a warmth that she felt reaching out from within her to join this new source. She held on to it, wanting to bask in this glow as long as she could. She opened her eyes. Colette and Joe had threaded their fingers together, hand in hand across the table from her, and Ren had reached out to add her energy to the fold.

FOUR

As Ren settled into daily life and begrudgingly accepted that there were chores and expectations, she realized she had been blessed with an amazing opportunity. It dawned on her that she could finally put her art history degree to some use. When it got down to facts, Delaney House was not much more than an elaborate storage facility for priceless wares. Between what Mariel had built in the name of the Delaney Society, and the private collection from Mariel's own adventures, Ren was face-to-face with a collection most amateur historians would kill to pore over. The private collection ran the gamut of cultural influences: Spanish, Italian, and Greek. It included other influences; so many that Ren's brain had trouble keeping up. All this on top of the fact that she was living inside a cornerstone of local history. The original mansion, lovingly referred to as Delaney House, was built in the early 1800s and still every bit as beautifully cared for as the day the last chandelier was hung under the watchful eye of William Delaney himself.

More than once, Ren had to stop and close her eyes, shuttering herself from the sensory overload of priceless treasures. The trove on display to the general public only consisted of the first three rooms. Large though they were, they didn't carry the impact they were meant to once the secret treasury hidden throughout the rest of the house was revealed. Even as time wore on, Ren was mystified: Mariel had foresight enough to plan and prepare for a lifetime. More than one really, as she has no idea how long this life was going to last. Ren had trouble planning a week in advance and Mariel had been establishing a treasury for herself and her family for over a hundred years now. Sometimes, she was allowed to move through the rooms, cataloguing and studying antiquities that had been boxed up and stored away decades before. Mariel had even admitted that she had forgotten what lie in a number of the boxes.

"Memory is a strange creature," Mariel mused, though Ren wasn't quite sure if she was actually part of the conversation, or just privy to it. "It can be nearly impossible to remember what you had for lunch just an hour after on some days." She laughed and Ren still wasn't sure if she should speak up. "But when you discovered your first love, that moment is locked tight. I can almost recount the specks of dust hovering in the air between us."

Ren stood in the doorway, ready to begin another grand adventure in another nameless room. She watched Mariel drift to the staircase. She turned, looking at Ren and for once; she wished Mariel had been talking to herself.

"No exploring today. It's First Thursday."

First Thursday, as the name suggested, was the first Thursday of the month. The doors of Delaney House were not only open to the public at large, but to the Daughters of the Revolution, another local historical society that met once a month to drink tea and gossip.

"Don't let the name fool you. It's pretty

much a sewing circle for rich widows." Joe had commented the first time Ren watched them file in. As she watched them file out later that day, she had many more colorful phrases to describe them.

"They're smarmy, vindictive, shallow —" Ren started, pacing the common room as Mariel and Colette watched.

"They donate a considerable amount to our museum," Colette interjected.

"They made fun of Ren's hair." Joe breezed to her sister's defense, gliding a tray of tea and snacks to the table. Ren nodded, pointing to Joe as if she made a very strong argument. Mariel could hardly suppress a smile.

"It's true," Ren slumped onto the couch. "They spent a half hour deciding which species of bird I resembled."

Everyone paused, the question looming in the air, no one wanting to say it out loud. Ren looked up from her melancholy, her eyes moving across the curious faces. She huffed and folded her arms, pursing her lips tight.

"They couldn't decide between a crowned crane and a kingfisher."

Joe raised her open hands in surrender as Ren gaped at her. Clearly, she hadn't expected Joe to sell her out so easily, but equally clear was Joe's inability to leave curiosity unsatisfied.

Mariel could hold back no longer as she poured a cup of tea and slid it closer to Ren.

"Unfortunately, Colette is right. We need someone donating to us so there is a paper trail to follow." She exhaled across the top of her teacup. "Otherwise, I would happily excuse them. Anything to rid us of Mrs. Abernathy."

There was a collective grimace at the name. Eunice Abernathy was the matron of the Daughters of the Revolution. She was also not a nice person, no matter what she pretended to be.

"She's hiding something. Probably dark magic." Inquisitive eyes were now on Josephine, who merely shrugged through further exposition. "She just seems the type. I'd guess sacrifices."

* * * *

Like previous Thursdays, Mrs. Abernathy shuffled slowly, her frail hips taking their toll on Ren's patience as the old woman moved toward the doors. Ren's mind compiled a list of options available to her to encourage Mrs. Abernathy's exit. None of the options were polite, nor did she suspect any of them would be well received when Mariel heard about it. She clenched her jaw and watched the grandfather clock's hand move slowly forward, matching the old woman's progress.

Again, the sewing circle had taken time to critique and criticize modern fashion, using Ren as their focal point. And again, it had taken everything Ren had to bite it back down and stay quiet. Ren stuck her tongue out, wrinkling her nose and doing everything in her power not to vocalize the responses brimming inside her. She loved her violent purple bangs and spikes, and saw nothing wrong with a bit of personal expression. Mariel said nothing against it either, and technically, she out ranked the lot of them.

For a moment, Ren considered screaming, knowing it wouldn't help move Mrs. Abernathy along, but thought it might pass the time for her. She could almost feel Mariel's cold, disappointed gaze, and decided it probably wasn't worth it. Her thoughts drifted back to the present and she realized that the old woman was still talking as she shuffled forward.

"Grandmother Abernathy, on my father's side, she knew William very well. Oh, but of course you know that. She's mentioned all throughout his diaries." She had been through quite a few of William's journals, but she had never come across any Abernathys. She wondered if it was more of the old woman's confusion surfacing, or if she was trying to impress Ren with false aristocracy.

She listened to the voice but not the words as the old bones shambled forward, taking ten more minutes to reach the doors. Ren looked at the floor, studying the pattern of the carpet, putting her mind anywhere but the present. Her fingers tingled with certainty, an assurance that she could easily shove the old woman down the stairs and out into the evening before any protest could be managed.

Again, Mariel's ghostly judgment lingered over her, driving back the impulse.

Finally, Mrs. Abernathy was four perfect feet away from the door, and Ren could not fight back the urge: she rushed around the old woman with too much fervor, and yanked the door wide. A gust barged into the room, startling them both and fluttering Ren's vibrant purple bangs as she held her post.

Mrs. Abernathy showed some life, almost jumping as the breeze pushed past her. She pulled her sweater tightly around her, as if by reflex, though Ren didn't consider it very cold, even for mid March.

"Gracious! You'd think that gust had been waiting all night for you to open that door."

For once, she said something Ren didn't feel the exhausting urge to roll her eyes at. She only smiled, nodding softly. She may have done both with too much enthusiasm, because Mrs. Abernathy turned toward her, squinting her eyes and adjusting her glasses. At first Ren thought it might have been a glare and wanted nothing more than to glare back, but the old woman just shook a finger and turned toward the door again.

"Pale, too pale," Mrs. Abernathy said to the room. "Looks like she's wasting away."

Ren's too-pale fingers tightened on the door handle, almost afraid she might slam the door closed before the old woman had a chance to pass through it completely. Ren tried to conceal the deep inhale that would turn into an exasperated sigh the moment the door's lock slid into a closed position. She watched the old woman turn and brace against the breeze, moving slowly down the steps of the porch and out into the evening world. Then, quietly as she was able, Ren slammed the door and twisted the lock, smiling with satisfaction as the bolt secured the door with a hard click. Mrs. Abernathy would not pass this way again tonight. Not for anything.

Ren let loose her exasperation loud and proud into the empty room. She pouted not having the satisfaction of sharing the moment with her sisters. She walked to the wall, switching off the main lights of the room. She would repeat herself for her sisters later. They owed her as much for leaving her alone tonight.

She moved through the showrooms, looking for obvious unsightliness from the day's visitors: greasy fingerprints on the glass cases, gum wrappers on the floor. She followed the tour path, letting her heels click on the wood, echoing softly in the room. She picked up around the main desk, arranging the brochures, turning down the rest of the lights as she made her way to the antechamber. As she passed through the great room, she looked up at the large painting on the mantle. A gilded frame held an elaborate rendering of William Delaney at the peak of life and health. He stood in an elegant waistcoat, top hat held to one hip, a gold pocket watch in the other hand. He stood proudly; his wide shoulders set back, his broad chest raised. He wore his hair in a side part, from left to right. It waved across his brow and rounded back over his ear. His nose was thin but proportionate and beneath it, his thick – woolly, even – moustache tapered to tail-like points at each end. Ren wondered at the artist and whether or not they had embellished the color or his hair. His hair and moustache seemed to radiate golden light. She smiled and admired the raw magnetism the portrait captured. She attributed it partly to his strong features: solid jaw, dark observant eyes, and a good square frame for a face. His eyes were what she always came back to. They stared off to the edge of the frame, across the room it seemed. Even though he was posing, she could tell he was still keenly observing. Silently, as she often did, she lamented not knowing him personally.

"Mrs. Abernathy implied that you were quite intimate with her Gram-gram, William," she smiled up at him as she sauntered past. "Is that something you hid in another journal I haven't read? Does General Delaney have a secret black book of dirty exploits?" She waited, giving him a moment to present his defense. When he didn't, she gently kissed her fingers and blew the lingering kiss up to his likeness.

"Goodnight, William. Try to stay out of trouble."

* * * *

Colette could feel the pressure against the bottom of her foot. It was an annoying insistence that meant someone was poking her with something. She kept the magazine up to her face, trying to ignore the nagging desire to snatch whatever it was and beat someone with it. She debated whether it was more likely to be Ren or Joe, and decided that they were really more like two sides of the same trouble-making coin. She tried to be grateful that it took a considerable amount of work to annoy her; Ren and Joe would probably be merciless if she were ticklish.

Her mind drifted back, as it often did, to her father and mother. Colette had been born with a 'congenital insensitivity to pain' as modern doctors diagnosed it. She couldn't feel pain at all. As a child in depression-era America however, her father called it – and her – a burden. She was lucky to have a mother who worried about her, even though it was probably too often. It was the single thing that separated her from so many children that didn't survive the disorder.

Her father made a good living as a salesman, often complaining that they'd be living a better life if they didn't have to spend so much time worrying about a child who didn't know better herself. When Black Monday struck, even his fast talk couldn't keep him from the bread line. He wasn't the first to go, or even the last; it all happened at once. The owners took their money and ran, cutting everyone loose in one short meeting. Everyone was on the street, looking for something new to survive on. Looking for somewhere that held the promise of a better tomorrow.

One day, her father packed up everything they had, and they drove off into the wilds, away from the city. They travelled through the disenchanted farmlands of America, offering 'Cure-all' elixirs and good luck charms to the unfortunate and downtrodden. Her father took advantage of anyone he could make a profit from, including his own daughter. Her mother protested at the beginning, trying to care for her daughter as she was meant to. Late at night, Colette would hear the arguments between her parents. In the morning, there was no sign of it, and her mother only looked more defeated as the days wore on. Eventually, she stopped protesting at all. She sat on the running board of their Model A, wearing an unconvincing smile while he continued to poison everything he touched, including their daughter.

As the poverty wore on across the country, people were harder to part from their money, even harder to part from their property. Schemers had to be quick, but they had to be convincing too. They had to be able to deliver before payment. The people wanted a show, a tell, and a promise that their money would not be wasted on clever lies. Colette was the ace up her father's sleeve, though it was hard for her to decide if it was ever good or not. She was no longer a burden, at least not by name. She was his star, even though she could see what it was doing to her mother. She worked every day to earn meals for her mother and herself. All she had to do was listen to her father deliver his speech, take a swig of his 'miracle tonic' and then walk in and out of a pile of hot coals in one of the community fire pits that every tent town had.

A community fire usually promised a decent crowd of its own. Her father's charisma and commanding voice would draw some stragglers, but Colette wandering through the camp would draw the rest. She was a teenage starlet; all brown curls and pretty bows. She had a beautiful blue dress that fit her perfectly; the only thing she was missing was a pair of fine shoes. Everyone noticed her bare feet, but they were always too polite to comment, at least till they watched the show.

Whenever she walked toward the crowd, she could feel the frills and folds play around her, urging her to dance. She wanted to dance so badly. The dress was so nice, it didn't feel right to just stand and do nothing in it, but her father wouldn't let her. He said one dress was quite enough for her and it would last longer if she didn't do anything unnecessarily, like dancing.

Eventually, though she tried to fight it, she receded like her mother. She knew there was a better life for her; somewhere far away from the tent towns and her father's schemes. She knew it was going to get harder before it got better, because one day she would have to leave. It would never be easy to leave her mother behind, and if she did, she knew her mother wouldn't survive long without her. Her curse was their livelihood. It seemed like the only time her mother showed any sort of life anymore was when she was wrapping Colette's feet after a demonstration, and then it was only sorrow.

Fortunately, she never had to figure out how to leave them. They were somewhere in Tennessee, she remembered the lush greens of the tobacco fields and all the farmhands tending them. They had been making good money in plenty of small towns on their way south. They had a strict routine: Wake up, trade in on misfortune, get on the road again. They would drive until dark, where they would camp for the night and look for another nearby town in the morning. They had stopped for the night somewhere along the highway, Colette and her mother in a tent along the roadside while her father slept in the car. He insisted that as long as there was a chance for anyone to cheat him, his car and his money would always be close by.

Unfortunately, the signs painted on the side identifying his 'miracle tonic' also easily identified the car. In the middle of the night, while she and her mother pretended to sleep, men came to collect a refund on his miracles. They mourned his passing quietly, hoping to remain unnoticed by the roadside. She never saw her father again, not even his remains. The strangers took everything: the car, her father, and all their worldly possessions. All they were left was the tent and their own clothes.

When morning broke, Colette knew they had to carry on. Her mother refused to budge from the floor of the tent. She stared off, listless and unresponsive. Nothing Colette could say or do would rouse her. After an hour, Colette knew she had to do something. She left her mother in the tent and began walking, looking for food or help or anything, really. She walked all day, the miles showing on her face and her feet, but found nothing. She slept fitfully that night, worried about her mother and if she'd ever find help to send back.

The next day, Colette experienced her first genuine miracle and hitched a ride on a farm truck. It took her all the way to the next shantytown, but no one there was in any position to offer her help. She couldn't feel the hunger, but she knew how long it had been since she'd eaten. She could feel the weakness in her limbs. Her remaining time was a blur of confusion and exhaustion, not really comprehending, but quite certain what was coming next.

Certainty had a funny way of disappointing her that day. Instead of pearly gates or a big black nothing, Colette instead found herself in the back of a covered carriage, being tended to by a young blonde woman with kind, sympathetic eyes and a miraculous story to tell.

Her story had remained mostly unknown to her sisters. They knew where and when she came from, but only Mariel knew the whole story. Only Mariel was there to find her. The other sisters occasionally noticed what might be considered resilience, but nothing truly remarkable. Colette had learned to be quite careful on her own, most of the time. Not until Ren and Joe saw her catch a pinky toe on the coffee table and barely stumble, much less carry on without so much as a single curse. She bowed to the storm of questions and gave them a brief explanation: that she had a condition that meant she couldn't feel pain. While she thought that was a solid end to the discussion, they heard the call of experimentation.

Some days, it was an annoyance without equal. Others, she couldn't help but be grateful for their uninhibited display of youth. Josephine was starting to lose the spark in recent years, as most of her sisters had. Colette often wondered if she ever had that spark, but sometimes, it could be drawn out of her. When Ren and Joe were together, it seemed to happen more often. There were times when it was easy to forget how old any of them were, and just live for the moment. Ren – not always, but often enough – spurred it.

Joyous youth or bored malcontent, Colette could never be certain, but she was certain that Ren's existence fought against the maturity level of the whole household.

She didn't even bother to lower her magazine. She grabbed the pillow tucked under her arm and threw it. She heard it cut through the air, announcing with a dull thud it had acquired its target. Colette smiled as Joe yelped.

"It's not me!"

Colette snapped the magazine down, locking eyes with Ren who hovered at the end of her footrest. Joe sat on folded legs huddled behind Colette's pillow a number of feet further on. Ren was motionless, holding a pencil pointed at the arch of Colette's foot. Slowly a Cheshire smile spread across her face. Perhaps Ren was trying to spread amusement; Colette fought a smile and tried to appear unamused.

"You realize that by doing this, by acting out, you are not only showing disrespect to me, but you are also disrespecting the house itself."

Ren and Joe pouted to each other. Ren looked around, her head rotating cartoonishly as she threw up her arms.

"Oh house! I beg your pardon!" She yelled at the ceiling, eyes as open as her mouth. "Colette ignores us, even when we try to be polite! It's our only recourse! It's not my fault; I am merely a product of my environment! I must do as I must!"

"No, you mustn't," Colette replied coolly, trying harder to fight a smile.

"But I must."

"No."

"Oui."

"Ren."

"Col–" she held onto the syllable, Colette's eyes narrowing. People had tried calling her "Col" over the years, and it grated at her. There were few things that bothered her more, including being experimented on by youthful sisters. "–ette."

She nodded satisfactorily. Ren would survive the day.

"Both of you, please, go find something else to do – something that doesn't involve me in any way, shape or form."

She raised her magazine again, opening it back to her place. She counted to five and then kicked out. She collided with something and Ren yelped, shaking her hand.

"I think you broke my finger!"

"You were warned."

Ren got up, huffing off toward the kitchen. Joe lingered for a moment.

"She didn't mean anything by it."

Colette lowered her magazine, her face softening toward Joe.

"Neither did I. Help her put some ice on it. It's probably just a sprain."

FIVE

Ren woke, stretching like a cat and twisting away from the bright sun. As good as it felt on her skin, her eyes argued that it was no good for her at all. Her joints resisted any motion that meant she was leaving the comfort of her bed, making it extra difficult to get her day started. When she was finally on her feet, they dragged, protesting every step.

She moved down the hall and took each step one at a time, yawning and still refusing to open her eyes any more than necessary. Hers were the only sounds she could hear, certain that the rest of her sisters were hibernating, quite possibly along with the entire city.

She shuffled her way to the kitchen, moving

past the tea cabinet without a second glance. It was too early for decisions. She needed the firm slap of a dark cup of coffee to get her started. Setting the coffee pot in the sink to fill, she opened the coffee tin; deeply inhaling and feeling the smile creep across her face, the only thing that hadn't dragged itself out this morning. She prepped the machine, double-checked that both grounds and water had been filled and turned the pot on.

Within minutes, the sweet scent of crème brûlée snaked out into the room, demanding to be noticed as the brew steamed itself into the pot. Ren smiled again, breathing deep. She leaned against the counter, biding her time until the first cup could be hers.

After a quiet cup all to herself, she decided she was awake enough to require company. She looked up at the clock on the wall, and then shrugged. She didn't actually care what time it was. If the sun was up and she was conscious, it was time to wake Joe.

She crept to the sleeping girl's door, then threw it open.

"Wake up, sleepyhead! Time to embrace the

life the gods blessed you with!" She yelled in a singsong, almost needing to cover her ears to seek refuge from her own voice. Josephine jumped, pushing herself away from the door defensively, then glared, collapsing back onto her pillows.

"I hate you so much." Her words might have carried more weight, if only she were conscious enough to put the effort behind them.

"Oh, you do not," Ren climbed onto the bed beside her, reaching out and gently depressing the girl's button nose, over and over. Joe's brow furrowed, her lips pouted, but she refused to open her eyes.

"Right! Wakey wakey!"

"Obviously, some of us didn't get as much deep rejuvenating sleep as others." Joe glared through slits, half of her face compressed against the pillow. One look told her that Ren was not going to quit until Joe was up and struggling with the day alongside her. She rolled her face into the pillow and screeched.

Colette's curly brown locks bounced past the open door, backpedalling long enough to glare with tired eyes into the room.

"All of this ruckus better mean breakfast is waiting downstairs."

Ren turned, smiling wide.

"I made coffee!"

Colette groaned, carrying forward.

Ren returned to the kitchen minutes later, limping along as she supported Joe to the table.

"Good morning, Colette," Ren said officially, Joe murmuring an echo. Both perked up at the same time, realizing that there were new smells in the kitchen. Colette had an egg on the stove, keeping one eye on it as she sliced a tomato. The toaster popped up at the other end of the counter, ejecting an English muffin. In the slow blink of Joe's sleepy eyes, Colette threw breakfast together and was already moving out of the room.

"Share and share alike, right?" Joe yawned as Ren set a cup of coffee in front of her.

"Not on your life. You want breakfast, make some."

"The location is less than exotic, and the service is less than stellar." Ren topped off her own cup. "I tell you Joe, there was nothing about any of this in the brochure."

Colette spoke around diminishing bites of breakfast. "There's a brochure?"

"Yeah, you know: 'Meet new and interesting people, see the world, live forever.'"

"There's an asterisk on that last part." Joe smiled, breathing her coffee rather than drink it.

Colette laughed. "You settled the fate of your soul on a brochure with an asterisk?"

"It was a really nice brochure. Glossy, even."

Colette finished her last bite and reached out, ruffling Ren's bedhead. The task appeared to take more effort than she would have thought, the hair moving very little and her fingers felt coated. Her hand moved to Ren's shoulder in a wiping motion.

"Less product, Ren. Hair needs to breathe."

"If I use less, it moves more."

"Hair is —" She held up a hand and turned. "Never mind. I'm going to take a shower. Start a kettle for Mariel. And make yourselves some breakfast. I'm not going to listen to you two whine all day."

"We're not going to whine *all day*."

"Don't you have some meeting to go to?"

"It's an estate sale. We're getting a sneak peek

because the dearly departed liked us."

Ren and Joe shared a glance, Ren deciding to confront the bad news head on. "And by 'we' you mean yourself in the royal person, right?"

"No, I mean you, you and me." She pointed at each of them, smiling. "I was going to wait till later to come back for you, but since you're both up, you might as well come with."

Joe's eyes returned to Ren, her jaw set. "I could still be sleeping, Ren."

"But you'd miss all the fun we're going to have."

"It doesn't sound like fun."

Colette leaned into the table, trying to sideline the conversation that was about to start. "I swear, if you two can just get dressed and behave long enough to help me with whatever we get at this sale, I'll take you to Royale."

Ren raised an eyebrow, uncertain what kind of offer was being put on the table. But any question she was about to ask was quickly cut off by Joe's instant acceptance and sudden alertness.

"Seriously? Tonight?"

"Yes, tonight. But I mean it – *best* behavior."

Ren looked back and forth, waiting for an

explanation. What she got was more of Joe's curious actions. This time, she jumped up from her seat and wrapped Colette in a deep hug.

"I promise! Oh god, what am I going to wear?" She spun and looked frantically at Ren. "What are *you* going to wear?"

"I don't even –"

Colette laughed and put an arm around Joe, trying to calm her.

"It's a night club. There's loud music and fancy drinks and lots and lots of sweaty people. For some reason, Joe loves going there."

Joe only jittered, her eyes somewhere else, her knuckles thumping against her chest. "It's the sound and the lights. You can *feel* the music there."

"Mariel has a hard line about doing anything that affects the reputation of the House, so we don't go very often. Even though I have made it perfectly clear that the people who come to the museum are hardly the people you find at a night club."

"Wait, Mariel goes to the club, too?"

"Oh no. It's not her thing at all. She'd be much happier at a gala. Club nights are usually for you youngin's."

Ren cringed. "I'll agree to anything, just don't ever say that word again."

Colette smiled and released Joe to her daydream. "Good. Get some breakfast and get dressed. We've got a long day and a longer night."

* * * *

Ren stepped onto the curb, turning to adjust her top in the reflection of the passenger side window. Colette didn't require them to be in professional dress, but she did ask Ren and Josephine to wear something "nice".

"The gentleman in charge of the estate's affairs is someone we regularly do business with. I would like to stay in his good graces."

On the car ride over, Joe and Ren discussed – loudly – whether Colette had meant it as a slight against their personalities or their sense of fashion. Really, they knew it was a simple statement that meant nothing more than the words spoken, but their intent hit home. Colette looked uncomfortably agitated the entire trip.

She rounded the car, appearing on the sidewalk next to them. She took a deep breath while they primped. Her brow crinkled as she watched them flank her.

"Please tell me we are done with the fun and games."

"Can I drive home?" Joe smiled, as if they games might resume any moment.

"Do you have a license?"

"No."

"Then no."

"But you don't have one either."

"But I am the responsible one."

Joe paused, her argument meeting a swift defeat against sound logic. She nodded, motioning for Colette to proceed. Colette took one look at Ren, who mimicked Joe's gesture, and moved up the sidewalk.

Ren and Joe followed quietly, not wanting to distract Colette. It was obvious that this meeting was important to her. They were surprised to see as they approached the front door, an elderly man of surprising haste came out and down the walk to meet them.

"Ah, Colette, my dear. Radiant as ever," He

smiled as he took her hand, kissing her on the cheek. He looked genuinely happy to see her, but it was obvious to them that he was anxious about something.

"Oh, Henry, you're too much. How are you?"

"Life is good to these old bones. Work keeps the spring in my step."

She smiled. "I brought along a couple of girls from the museum to help out today. This is Florence. And Josephine." He took each of their hands delicately, smiling warmly and looking each pleasantly in the eye. He was almost hypnotic with his approach that Ren forgot to cringe at her birth name.

"A pleasure to meet you both."

Colette took his attention right back, taking him by the hand and resuming the walk up to the door.

"I could barely wait for my appointment time this morning. I'm eager to see what surprises you have inside –"

Henry stopped and for a moment looked very old and frail. He smiled again, but this was not the warmth he just gave to each of them. It was a smile that meant he was trying to soften bad news.

"I am sorry that I didn't call sooner. I am afraid I need to ask you to reschedule your appointment."

Colette looked shocked, almost betrayed by the words. "I don't understand."

"Another of my client's has put me in a bind and is currently occupying the house. She has insisted that she have first look at the lot and is not going to budge until she has been over every item." It was becoming apparent that this was not only a shameful admission, but it was an annoyance to him as well. "If we could simply reschedule, I will hold all other clients until after you have had your turn."

For a moment, Colette appeared wounded. Someone that she obviously considered to be a friend had slighted her – worse, it was completely by surprise. But having spent plenty of time with Mariel, it only took a moment for that look to fade, replaced by a calm exterior. The only indicator of her displeasure now was the visible tension in her jaw muscles.

"It's fine. We'll do it however you need to,

Henry," he visibly relaxed. "Though I do need to know who is stirring up trouble in our friendly community."

His jaw dropped and he stammered. He looked back at the door, and then to Colette.

"Henry, be reasonable. Whoever it is, we can easily run them out of town. You, Mariel, the other preservationists, myself…"

"It's just not that simple, Colette."

Her jaw tensed. "Henry, who is in there?"

As if on cue, Ren saw a flutter of curtains from the front window, instinctively, she prodded Joe for her attention. They both squinted, hoping to see something that would solve the mystery. The curtain fluttered back too far, revealing the spy, though it was impossible to tell if the reveal was on purpose or accidental. But both girls clearly saw those bitter eyes peering out at them. Ren couldn't see clear enough, but it almost seemed like she was smiling.

"No way."

Colette turned to both of them. "What?"

They pointed at the window, but the curtain had already fallen back into place. "It's her."

Colette looked at the house, then to Henry, and then turned back to them.

"Her who?"

Ren spit out the name like a bitter taste.

"Abernathy."

* * * *

Mariel had just finished the morning's business and moved herself to the common room. A fresh cup of breakfast tea steeped on the table in front of her as she sat back in her chair, ready to peruse the morning paper. She heard the satisfying creak of the joints in her chair and smiled. 'Her chair' was not a loving moniker she had adorned it with – it was actually hers. It had been a present from William in another time – another world, really.

It was a high-back rocker in dark wood – rosewood, if she remembered correctly – with thick, sloping blades and large ornate arms. It was almost therapeutic to listen to it roll back and forth on the floor beneath her, the heft of the chair making a deceptively heavy sound, completely unlike other rocking chairs. She would often come to sit and rock, listening to it and imagining her troubles crushed underfoot.

The upholstery was nothing close to authentic any longer. Mariel had long given up on historical propriety in this one instance, and though she had been chastised a number of times for jeopardizing the value of the piece, every time she sank into the plush cushions she had chosen over the stuffy, unforgiving historically accurate ones, she knew she made the right choice. Kind as she was in her daily life, Mariel was a cruel mistress when it came to her quiet moments and had gone through a number of restorations done to the chair. She thought of this one as *Her Chair, Mk. IV.*

She traced a finger over the wood, marveling at how it still seemed to burn with an inner light, like embers just beneath the veneer. She might have to bend a rule and make sure to revisit them when the chair needed adjustments again. Maybe she'd even change the color scheme. The French vanilla still popped against the dark wood, but it showed age all too easily. Maybe next time, she'd consider –

The door burst open through the kitchen and

she knew that her moment's peace was gone. What she could not have been ready for was two young women looking almost professional and openly bickering as they raced across the room toward her.

"I'm going to tell her!"

"No, I am! I called dibs!"

"You can't call dibs on this! You had shotgun last!"

"You can have dibs *and* shotgun!"

"By cheating!"

"Am not!"

They shoved each other, picking up speed as they raced closer. Her survival instinct kicked in and begged her to move away from the chair; to hurry and lock herself safely away behind closed doors. Instead, she took a long slow blink and a deep breath as the chaos stormed toward her. She raised her arms up, palms out, pleasantly surprised to see that the motion seemed to calm and quiet them some.

Under the veil of confusion, she had to fight down a tickle of amusement. These two girls were anxious, betraying their age with an enthusiasm she secretly hoped they would never outgrow – but would like to see them control better.

"There is news, I presume?" They both opened their mouths and she held up a hand. "One at a time, please. Josephine."

As if Mariel were not right there, in full view and looking directly at them, Joe threw an elbow and gave Ren a playful jab. Ren's jab was less playful, and Joe had to catch her breath before she could speak.

"So we were going with Colette to meet Harry –"

"Henry." Ren chimed in.

"Yes, Henry, over at some estate to look everything over. But before we could go in, he came out to greet us."

"More like bounce us." Ren growled. Joe threw another elbow in an attempt to quell the commentary.

"I'm getting to that."

"What do you mean 'bounce'?" Mariel asked, rising from her chair. She didn't like the way this story was going and she wanted to skip to the end quickly. "He moved the appointment?"

"Someone got to him first."

Colette and Mariel shared a glance as Colette entered the room.

"Eunice Abernathy got there ahead of us and charmed her way into our appointment time."

Ren and Joe deflated, Colette having told the best part of the story and ruining their surprise. Mariel shook her fists, pacing out into the room.

"How did she get in before us? Why?"

"I don't know. She's got to be looking for something."

Mariel growled out loud, a display that neither Ren nor Joe was ready for. "Would it be so much to ask her to just grow old and die quietly?"

Again they were thrown. This side of Mariel was completely unknown to them. It was equal parts intimidating and troubling. Neither decided to point it out. Mariel wandered a slow angry circle before opening her office and disappearing inside. Colette moved to the table, grabbing the mug of tea and giving her sisters a consolatory smile.

"She'll be alright. Mrs. Abernathy has always been kind of a thorn."

Ren nodded, she could understand already.

Colette backed away from them slowly, talking as she moved toward the office door.

"A deal's a deal. We're going out tonight, but you're going to owe me a day of servitude."

They smiled at her, nodding emphatically as they tittered in place. The moment the door closed, they both exploded in excitement, squealing at each other as they raced upstairs to decide on outfits for their evening.

* * * *

Ren and Joe skipped hand in hand out onto the dance floor. They left Colette at the bar, not wanting to appear suspicious by hovering. By genetics or just her own maturity, Colette was rarely questioned in cases where an ID might clarify things. It wasn't that they didn't have them, they just weren't authentic and the fewer questions aroused, the less attention they brought to themselves and their cover.

Colette was already a memory as they followed the throbbing bass into the lights and churning bodies. It was a liberating feeling to be able to cut loose and, for just a little while, pretend to be like everyone else. She twirled with Joe, catching bursts of light from the ceiling reflecting in her sister's eyes. She needed this. She needed to be among people and the sensations of life. As much as Ren loved the books and antiques, they reflected her unique situation. Something she needed to forget every once in a while. She battled with her feelings from time to time, still not fully over leaving her old life behind. She had to accept the fact that she was something different, that she might outlast everything she knew.

But it wouldn't be alone.

She smiled genuinely as Joe threw her arms up and spun around. On the dance floor, they didn't need to pretend. They were anonymous, forgettable. They could be themselves and not worry about pretenses and remembering their place. They could blend and just be.

Josephine's face changed as they danced, a little less joy in her eyes. Before Ren could figure out why, she felt it. Someone had their hands on Ren's hips, pressing up against her from behind. A fire caught inside her. There was an amount of respect she insisted upon from her fellow man.

She didn't demand much from people, but she believed in certain unwritten rules. One was that a gentleman should always ask permission.

She turned as Joe reached out for her. Ren made a move to brush her hand away as she completed the turn. She could already feel Mariel's disapproval settling over her, and she didn't care. This was justified. She glared into the chest of a man more than a head taller than her. He was toned, and the smile on his face told her that he was accustomed to getting what he wanted. She continued to glare; making her way up to his eyes, wishing the cold stare could do more than just show disapproval. He seemed to take the turn as an invitation, sliding his hands further around her waist. Reaching back with her own slender fingers, she found two thick thumbs and grabbed them, bending as she watched his smile turn to a grimace. Her wrists twisted, and he seemed to dance on his toes, trying to bend out of the pain. As her hands rose, his body lowered; her gaze was met a look of fear and apology reflecting in his wide eyes.

Her head snapped to the side, ready to confront someone else as she felt a hand alight her shoulder. Joe's worried brow softened her steel grip and she let him go.

Ren let Joe guide her away from the dance floor, toward a mostly empty table where Colette was guarding their seats. She sipped her drink, an eyebrow raised.

Ren mounted the stool, holding up a finger for everyone to wait while she took a long pause to empty her drink. She gasped for air, putting the glass back down on the table and looked in Colette's direction.

"Go ahead, say it."

Colette set her glass down, certain of a number of things she could say, and knowing most of the responses that would come from them.

"Are you alright?"

Ren began to inhale, ready for the argument to start. She paused and let the words repeat themselves in her head. It was a loud place but there was no way to mishear that. There was also no way to mistake the look of concern on Colette's face. Joe leaned over to her, jabbing her in the ribs. Ren had forgotten to exhale. Her eyes met Colette's again and the raised eyebrow was joined with a smirk.

"Are you alright?" She repeated, a little louder and more exaggerated. Ren could almost feel the sarcasm. She couldn't help but smile in reply. Colette leaned in. "Just be careful, they're not always so easy to handle."

Ren nodded, certain that was true and hoped she would never have to find out.

The rest of the night went on as if nothing had happened. They spent most of the evening on the dance floor as if they were limitless. Ren and Joe both taking turns with bouts of giggles, proving that the alcohol had gotten to them more than Colette, but the eldest sister had been pacing herself. Even so, by closing time, they had burned off most of the alcohol on the dance floor.

The walk home was quiet. They travelled arm in arm in arm, a trio of heels clicking in unison on the empty city streets.

"You guys might have to carry me up to my room when we get home," Ren leaned her head on Joe as they walked. Joe shrugged her off.

"You can forget that, I'm going to have enough trouble getting myself upstairs – and out of this dress – much less worrying about you." Colette laughed, the sound echoing off the tall buildings around them.

"Just leave me on the couch, I'll change in the morning."

Neither Ren nor Joe had a reply, they both looked left to the sister keeping them from stumbling off the curb. The three shared another laugh, almost enjoying the walk home as much as the night out; so much that they barely registered the car pulling alongside them.

"Hey!"

Colette waved the car along, not bothering to look.

"Oh no," Ren whispered. "Is it –"

"Shh," Colette gave Ren's hand a squeeze. "It's fine."

The car came to a halt and the door opened. Colette put her other hand on Ren's to steady her, hoping that Joe would follow suit.

"Hey! I'm talking to you, goth bitch!" His words were thick, it sounded as if he'd been drinking.

Colette stopped, hanging her head in disappointment. Ren and Joe looked at her, then at each other. Colette turned first.

"I'm starting to understand why she had to resort to violence in the first place."

Even at a distance, they could see that he was bigger than any of them, but he was having trouble standing still. There was a list in his stance. He had definitely drunk more than necessary tonight.

"I'm not talking to you," He pointed at Colette, then drawing an invisible line, stopped at Ren. "I'm talking to *you*. You need to apologize."

The trepidation that had been building up inside her quickly evaporated to anger. *Apologize?*

She stepped forward and clenched her fists. "For what, not letting you molest me back there?"

"Don't know what's wrong with you. Ladies love Nico."

"What?"

"I said, 'Ladies love Nico.'" He almost danced as he said it again.

"Yeah, but I don't —" the pieces clicked for Ren just a moment too late. The reaction was a combination of laughter and choking on the rest of her words. "Oh god. *You're* Nico."

He made a grunt that she took as affirmation as he gestured to unheard applause. None of them were certain if this was an alcohol related response or if it might have just been him.

"Wow." Ren turned back to her sisters. "I've heard enough for one night. Can we go home?"

She had barely taken a step when he grabbed her hair, tugging her back and making her cry out.

"You're not going anywhere till you apologize, bitch," Nico spun her to face him and she lashed out, spitting in his eyes and kicking at him. Her fury was silenced when she saw the knife glint off the streetlights.

His eyes glittered almost as much as the blade. Nico wanted her to see what he was doing. He held it out in the open for her to see clearly, and then tightened his grip on her hair as he brought it in closer. Instinct took over and Ren quieted, waiting to see what came next.

"I think you need to put that away," Colette spoke, closer than he would have liked her to be. He swung the knife in her direction.

"Back up, unless you want some too."

Ren wanted to put the attention back on her,

to get Colette out of harm's way. But before she could, Colette smiled. She smiled and stepped closer. Nico's knife hand wavered, and Colette put out her palm, closing her hand over the knife. Ren could see him sober instantly as he released her and backed away. She smiled for a full second before she started to panic right with him.

Colette continued to smile, her hand outstretched, Nico's knife sticking through her palm. Ren's stomach turned as Joe came up behind her, hugging her and watching with her sisters as he stumbled backward and ran for his car. Colette kept waving as he sped past them, the car swerving wildly down the street.

When he was out of sight, she pulled the blade free and handed it to Ren. Ren dropped it into her purse.

"Can we go home *now*?" Joe said with a sigh as she wrapped her jacket around Colette's hand.

Ren and Joe flanked their sister as they began to walk again.

"You're a little scary, you know that, right?" Ren whispered softly as they walked.

"I love you too, Ren."

"You are both grounded," Joe huffed as she

held the jacket tight around Colette's hand. "And Ren, you owe me a new jacket."

SIX

Ren sat at tea time the next day feeling a bit like she was in detention. Mariel said nothing. She didn't even look in Ren's direction. Of course Colette told her about last night. It was hard to pass off a bandage and a hole in the hand like "oh, nothing." So not only did Mariel know, but she also knew it was all Ren's fault. She gulped, trying to swallow her guilt with the first sip of apple spice. She almost dumped the whole cup down her shirt when Mariel finally broke the silence.

"Colette told me what happened," Mariel spoke first, making eye contact with Ren second. "Don't blame her."

Ren looked surprised. Blame her? How could

she? She shook her head.

"No, never." Ren smiled, putting a hand on Colette's knee.

"Good," Mariel smiled. "Because the two of you," she gestured to Ren and Joe, "have a new task ahead of you."

They both sat forward, registering each other's surprise.

"You are both to start taking defense classes. The next time trouble arises, I want you adequately prepared to handle it." She looked at Ren as she said it. "Bravado will only take you so far."

"So, what are we learning?"

* * * *

Ren sat on the sidelines, her own trepidation forgotten as she tried – and failed – to stifle her laughter while Josephine yelped and slid across the floor on her back. Trepidation rounded back to her as Mariel turned to her and took a fighter's stance.

It had been three, maybe four moves before Joe was spun around and slid out of the sparring area. It was hard to tell, Mariel moved *fast*. Faster than anyone might assume a woman of grace and propriety might move, anyway.

Ren turned, hoping to see someone else Mariel might have been gesturing to. The rest of the people in the gym were busy with their own workouts. No one seemed to care that Ren was about to be pummeled by a living piece of history.

She took a deep breath and stepped over the blue line that separated contenders from spectators. Her hands went up, and she tried to think of the long list of tips Mariel had given her and Joe over the past week.

What did she say? Arms in front of you, elbows at your side, feet at the –

Mariel shuffled her feet, darting forward and sweeping Ren's legs out from under her before she registered what was happening. She hit the padded floor, her spine crackling all the way down as her wind abandoned her.

- at the ready. Damn. Ren took the hand extended to her and hoisted herself back up to her feet. She shook off the temporary dizziness and tried to focus. The hands came up again and

this time, Ren cleared her mind. She focused on Mariel.

Her blonde tresses were tied in a topknot; only a few wisps were out of place as she stood at the ready. Her gi draped perfectly. When Mariel moved, it moved with her, not straining against her body like Ren's yoga pants and tank top. If she actually started getting into this she'd –

Ren saw Mariel kick, but it was too late, she was already moving when Ren reacted. She tried to put her leg up, to deflect the kick, or at least lessen the pain. Mariel twisted with the kick, letting it land, her body still turning. Again, she reacted too late to prevent it, but Ren tried to soften the blow by getting her forearms in the way of Mariel's impending fists. She winced against the impact, then felt her arms cast aside. Mariel smiled as she grabbed the straps of Ren's tank top. Panic fluttered under her purple bangs, she had no defense against being hurled across the ring.

Time slowed down as Mariel pulled back, building momentum. First, Mariel leapt in a decided direction, then, like a poor coyote tied to a boulder, Ren knew she would come hurtling after Mariel once the slack ran out. There was more of a tell in this motion, however. She saw it happen as a chain reaction. Mariel shifted her weight, muscles tensed and her fingers tightened on Ren's clothing, then her face changed. Her jaw tightened and her eyes brightened a little. Ren wondered if she wasn't just a little sadistic using this as a first full lesson. She wondered if she wasn't a little masochistic herself for going along with it.

Her body fell into the undertow of momentum, and desperation took over.

Ren's brain had accepted that this was going to happen; her body decided that one last effort was in order. As she passed Mariel, her hands instinctively latched onto the gi. A leg went out awkwardly, seeking a counterbalance against the inertia. The new information combined with the process already in motion shifted the balance and turned Ren into a pinion, pulling Mariel into a dance with her. Mariel was surprised, but only momentarily. She matched the movement, getting around it and taking them for another turn on the mat.

Ren's feet shuffled underneath her. Her

shoulders were being pulled far past her center of gravity and the only thing holding her up was her handhold on Mariel's uniform. She tightened her grip, trying to keep up with the momentum. Mariel braced her feet and stopped moving. Ren held fast, mostly, her body circling Mariel's until she twisted her way to the floor. She looked up sheepishly at her instructor, as Mariel straightened her uniform.

She kneeled next to Ren with a small chuckle. "That was good. You have it in your heart to be very good."

"But?" Ren added. Because there always was one.

"But you need to get your head involved. You need discipline."

Ren nodded. That was a chief complaint throughout her life. She was too impulsive; she needed to think more. Her mouth twisted as she considered it.

"Are you sure I wouldn't be better with a sword? Or a gun, maybe?"

Mariel shook her head. "Weapons come later. You need to be able to defend yourself *by* yourself first. Be your own weapon."

"And then guns?"

Ren got her feet underneath herself as Mariel helped her up. "Guns require registration. Bows however, are relatively easy to acquire. If you ask Colette very nicely, she might train you. She is exceptionally good."

Ren's brow creased upward, she would not have expected unassuming Colette to be their resident Robin Hood.

Joe chimed in now, delightfully curious. "And we start with swords when?"

Mariel clapped her hands, gesturing to both girls.

"Let us start again – with the basics."

* * * *

In the quiet moments she had to herself, Ren tried not to dwell too long on the unanswerable questions regarding her new existence. It did invade her thoughts from time to time. Realistically, at twenty-two years old, she had already cornered the market on omnipotence and invincibility – or so she'd believed. Those two false powers had been stripped away and she had been handed something very real – a second chance.

Try as she might to avoid it, Ren couldn't help but wonder what the rules were. What was her new lifespan? Was she really immortal, or just invulnerable to old age? If she died again, would she come back, or was this it?

She pulled a box down from the shelf and groaned. Her body healed faster now, that was the story. Unfortunately, the pain of healing was still just as awful as before. The abuse she took during training with Joe and Mariel was, like most things these days, nothing she had experienced previously. She was getting the hang of it though.

What Ren lacked in raw power, she made up for with her awareness. She could see the attacks coming in time to defend against them, though the actual act of defending required further practice, as evident from the screaming muscles and bruises all over her body.

As fast as her body might heal now, it was not fast enough for her liking. Ren was beginning to realize that even with forever stretched out before her, patience was not her virtue. Especially in the face of the stories and movies she'd seen.

Immortality was supposed to be exciting, sexy, perhaps accompanied by a soundtrack. When she thought about what she might be missing in her early years as an immortal, her patience hung on her like a lead-lined jacket.

She shook her head in a private dismissal and clenched her teeth as she lifted the box to the work desk. Life was not always boring. In fact, the days passed pretty quickly. She had her work, her sisters, an occasional nightlife, and a working knowledge of tea that was turning into an addiction.

No, it wasn't what the stories promised her, but it was better than the alternative.

A growl from downstairs called her attention. She stepped out to the railing to see Joe sprawled dramatically across the couch. She lifted herself up, tugging a pillow out from underneath her and held it over her face, screaming into it.

Ren rested her elbows on the railing, smiling down at the display.

"No one can hear your drama if you're going to scream it all into the pillow."

Joe's eye peeked out over the pillow and glared at her. She mumbled loudly into the pillow again. Ren still had no idea what she was saying, but by the tone, she could take a guess.

"Look, if you're going to suffocate yourself, be my guest. But do it quietly, some of us are working."

Joe threw the pillow at her. It was nowhere near its target and they both watched it arc and flop in the middle of the common area.

"You're not funny, Ren."

"You're right, I'm hilarious."

Ren waited in the silence for a moment, then gripped the railing to push herself back toward her work. Joe growled loudly again and pounded her fist on the back of the couch.

"I don't know why we put up with these visitors. Every season, they seem to get worse. They are terrible people!" She clenched her fists, as if she was begging Ren to understand her position. Ren nodded sympathetically. She had no previous season for comparison, but she was all too aware already.

"Somewhere between the mentally vacant and the young boys with no boundaries, there has to be a balance."

"We just have to tough out the season, Joe.

You said so yourself: everything will get back to normal once summer is over."

Joe sat up, waving a finger.

"That was long before the rotten little urchin, in his perfect little scout outfit and wholesome smile," Joe seethed until she lost her train of thought. She doubled back, stoking her anger again. "Oh, he was so polite with his questions, until no one was looking. He kept flipping up my skirt, Ren!"

Ren smiled, trying to nod appreciatively at the story. Inwardly, she was shaking her head at the theatrics, in spite of understanding her sister's frustration.

"He needs to have his merit badges reexamined, because I'm pretty sure that somewhere in the rulebook, it says you're not supposed to get handsy."

There was no fighting her laughter now. She almost doubled over, catching herself before she tumbled down the staircase. She pulled herself back up to the railing, making sure she was secure and balanced before carrying on.

"Handsy?" She wiped tears from her eyes, continuing the conversation through the spaces in the rails.

Joe's face burned with a mixture of frustration and embarrassment.

"He grabbed my ass, Ren," she almost yelled it. "Like he was testing melons!"

"Maybe if he was taller, he would have done that instead."

Joe paused, her eyes lighting with recognition and she threw another pillow in Ren's direction. This one came considerably closer to the mark.

"You're awful. I am seriously traumatized and you're making jokes."

Ren collected herself and sauntered down the stairs, slowly making her way to the couch. She folded her arms around her sister, cradling her and kissed her on top of her head.

"Did he at least promise to call?"

Joe huffed, pushing herself from the embrace, doing her best to storm out of the room with what remained of her dignity.

"Fine. If you're not going to show me a little respect, I'm going to cry my troubles into a hot pocket."

"Ugh! How can you eat those?"

"Because they're delicious."

"There's something wrong with your taste buds."

"Someone's taste buds are faulty?" Colette walked out of the Mariel's office; she was reading from a notepad as she weaved around them.

"I just said I was going to have a hot pocket," the fight had begun to leave Joe.

Colette made a sound of disgust as she headed toward the kitchen.

"That's exactly what I said!"

"Both of you shut up!"

Ren followed the two women into the kitchen. Colette was filling the teakettle with water, the notepad never leaving her field of vision. Joe was weighing her options in the freezer.

"Going alright out there today?" Colette momentarily looked between the other two.

"Mostly. Good crowd. Joe's been flirting."

"I have not! Ask Mariel."

Colette raised an eyebrow at Ren, who suppressed a laugh and waved off the impending conversation. They both watched quietly with a mixture of fascination and horror as Joe prepared her hot pocket.

"I know Mariel hasn't mentioned it yet, so I want to prepare you," Colette put the notepad down, directing her attention to Ren and Joe. "She'll explain better when the time comes, but you're going to be on your own for a while. Mariel's needed out west and I'll be going with her."

"You're kidding, right?" Joe was stunned; ignoring the beep that meant the microwave was done nuking her meal. "How long?"

She shrugged a reply. "She hasn't told me much, just that it's going to happen."

Ren looked between them, feeling like she missed something vital.

"So the two of us have to run this whole place? Alone?"

Suddenly, the implications were all too clear. She felt a panic settling in. She didn't want to be alone again.

A hand on hers broke the spell. Ren looked up and met Colette's warm eyes.

"The two of you can handle this; you practically run the place already." She turned to Joe. "Stop freaking out, you're going to be fine."

"Is someone getting moved?"

Colette shook her head. "Don't get your hopes up. It's hardly time for that yet."

"Can we have the twins?"

Ren's eyes bounced back and forth, following the conversation as she waited for one to best the other at this back and forth.

"I just said –"

"I know what you said, but can we?"

"We aren't even –"

Joe grabbed Ren, squeezing her cheeks as she held her sister captive. "But look at this face. This is a face that has obviously not experienced the twins yet."

There was a hesitation, then a smirk from Colette.

"That's a yes, isn't it?"

Colette turned to the teakettle, pulling it from the stove; it had started issuing steam but she beat it to the whistle and poured a cup.

"It's probably not going to happen, either way."

"Then I call dibs." Joe was insistent, and Ren was still lost.

"Fine, you have dibs," Colette looked at Ren for a moment, then back to Joe. "You think she's ready to meet them?"

Joe forced Ren's head to nod emphatically. Colette grabbed her notepad and her teacup and started to leave the room.

"It's on your head if they pull another Sophie."

Ren stood there, a flurry of new and confusing information twisting around her brain.

Twins? Sophie? Mariel and Colette leaving the house to Joe and herself? What was going on? She turned slowly to ask Joe, but she was already skipping out of the room, audibly relishing the first taste of her microwaved treat.

* * * *

Ren busied herself in the upstairs rooms, examining the content manifests of boxes and making sure that nothing was unaccounted for or had gone amiss. She was almost certain it was some kind of arduous hazing, like an antique snipe hunt. At some point, she was certain to discover a manifest with some unaccounted for item, and the search would begin. Only after days or weeks of searching and questions and queries and – if the plan was good enough – teetering on the edge of madness, it would be revealed with laughter and party poppers that the whole thing had been an elaborate ruse. They would explain it and Ren would feel sheepish and embarrassed and everyone would say that this time was even better than the time so-and-so fell for it.

Well, Ren decided, if anything was missing on the content labels, she would keep it to herself for until she had time to investigate privately, just to be sure.

Days had already been invested in the room's audit, and she was barely a quarter through. It took time to unpack and repack each box, making sure that the contents were as safe going back on the shelf as they were coming off it. And then there was the time lost cooing over some of the items she had discovered.

Old photographs and engineering schematics. Letters from a number of time periods: some to lovers, some to family, and some to no one in particular. Blankets and glassware and all manner of trinkets could be found in the boxes, most of them in remarkable condition. But what fascinated her most were the books. There were so many books; various printings of all manner of published manuscripts. She loved the journals most of all. She couldn't stop herself from diving in and reading cover to cover. She was always saddened when she was finished, doubly so if the words ended before the pages ran out. The insight they gave into the life of the author sometimes made her want to cry.

Secret lives, secret thoughts, she thought to herself. It was too late to offer them the ear or shoulder they might have needed in life, but she held them in her thoughts as she absorbed every word.

Ren had almost completely forgotten her paranoia when suspicion reared its ugly head.

It seemed too perfect not to be part of a trick. It was a dusty old box on the bottom shelf all the way at the back of the room. She spent the better part of the day going through the box, reading mostly, when she noticed the last line item was unaccounted for. Upon closer inspection, she noticed that it had been crossed off with one quick line that barely made it through the first few letters of the title. The pen had run out of ink, because the line continued to crease the paper across the rest of the title almost imperceptibly. She smiled, certain that this must be the snipe hunt she was looking for. On top of the shady way it was crossed out, it was the title that made her most suspicious:

The Personal and Private Reflections of Gen. William Delaney, 1856 —

She looked through the box a second time as she repacked it, confirming that it definitely was not there. Why would one of William's journals be in these boxes?

Shouldn't it be in the display case with the rest of his books? She shook her head and made a mental note and stashed the box back where she found it.

* * * *

Ren sat quietly, polishing the silver she had pulled from the cabinet. She tried to pretend that the job was far more important than it was. It was busy work while she tended to the empty museum, doubtful that anyone was going to come in at all. Unless there was a special circumstance, Delaney House was only open to the public a few hours a day. The schedule was designed to keep expenses at a minimum. Unfortunately, some days it seemed to keep visitors at a minimum too, as most visitors only appeared on the weekends.

The downtime allowed her to get time consuming jobs done without interruption, but those interruptions meant that she was doing something much more important than maintaining the silverware. When Delaney House had a visitor, it kept history from its own death in obscurity. William Delaney and countless others marched back out into the world, carried on a new memory. It meant that for just a while longer, these souls would not be forgotten.

She looked down, practically able to see her reflection in the rough surface of the worn service tray. She handled the dining set piece by piece in cotton gloves, resetting the display gently and closing the cabinet.

She cleared her throat, ready to usher her displeasure into the room and stopped, remembering she was alone. When she had an audience, Ren complained loudly, but it was more game than sincerity – at least she hoped that was how she conveyed it. She didn't like the act of simply agreeing, it was too smooth. Ren liked her chaos. She liked getting a reaction before she cooperated fully. She had no problem participating in the house, even if it dragged sometimes.

She didn't even mind the chores, though she'd be hard pressed to admit that out loud. Ren considered it a small gesture to show her appreciation to the souls they helped memorialize.

She placed the key in the lock of the cabinet and gave it a delicate twist. She wiped at the glass front and admired her handiwork. For at least another month or two, time would be held off the objects inside the cabinet. She turned to the room while she decided what to tackle next.

When the day's work was done, Ren retreated to the living area behind the large oak door. It was similar to the front door, though nothing as ornate. It was sturdy. Even on balanced hinges, she could feel the weight as she pushed the door open. Often, she wondered if the heavy door was a measure of security for the people living in these rooms, or for the treasures within them.

Ren never bothered to pose the question out loud.

As the door swung open, it swirled the air silently. The sudden gust twisted, pulling a delicious scent past her nose. She sniffed at the air again, a cornucopia of scents mingling, each breath harnessing something new. It made her think of home cooked meals, of Sunday dinners with family. The door all but forgotten, not completely open as she pushed past it with an eyebrow raised while she moved into the room.

A table was set up in the middle of the common room. The rest of the furniture had been pushed to the walls. Four chairs surrounded it. The room was full of sounds, noises tumbling into the makeshift dining area from the kitchen. It sounded like the rest of her sisters had their work cut out for them.

"No no no, once they are mashed, it's more of a whipping motion," She heard Colette instructing – that was the word, she sounded like a teacher. "The down force doesn't do anything once – yes! Like that!"

Ren poked her head around the corner to see Joe working up a sweat as she toiled over what appeared to be mashed potatoes. Colette was simultaneously scattering veggies into a bowl of lettuce and tossing asparagus around in a sizzling pan. Mariel had her head down, and a hand in the oven. The whole room smelled delicious.

"What the hell?" She couldn't help herself. For all the communal activities that had gone on in the house, she had never seen anything like this.

"Run, Ren! Save yourself! Before they force you into slavery too!" Joe smiled, confined to the corner of the kitchen as she tried to assist while staying out of the way.

Mariel closed the oven, a smile on her face that spoke of memories made long ago.

"Florence, if you please," she gestured to the cabinets. "Service for four, and then help Josephine choose a bottle of wine from the cellar."

They exchanged a glance. Joe mouthed the words again, as if being charged with the holiest of holy deeds. Joe's stunned silence was only met with Ren's confusion, then, they traded expressions.

Mariel smiled. "We have a tradition.

Everyone gathers for one last family dinner before someone leaves the house. Everyone eats and drinks and we make sure that we all go to bed full of food and laughter. It's how we all stay sisters, even when we don't see eye to eye." Her eyes lingered on Ren. She found herself smiling softly in reply, as Joe pushed her way out of the kitchen, making a mad dash for the cellar.

* * * *

What food remained had been put away and now there were only four women laughing, sharing stories and amassing a collection of wine bottles in the center of the table between them. For Ren, it felt like a night out with the girls, and she understood perfectly: She would never hate these women, they were her sisters. Now and forever, pretty much.

Colette distributed the remains of the final bottle among the four glasses and held hers high.

"To each of us: old, new and in-between. May we never be too long from a reunion."

Three glasses joined hers, clinking loudly.

Mariel stood, still moving in her usual

graceful measures, although Ren would not have believed it after this evening.

"My ladies, my beautiful wonderful ladies, that we might do this all night, but it is time we were all off to bed." Joe, who was both the first to rise and the closest, was pulled in for an all-enveloping hug. It surprised Ren to see the facade fall away and witness this heartfelt gesture. Ren stood, her head suddenly woozy and her legs wobbly. Her legs had that "like new" quality they did when she first arrived. She was oddly fascinated by it, blaming the tranquilizing effects of the wine on her comely reaction. She leaned just a bit too far slipping around her chair. Colette was there, sharing a giggle as they held onto each other for a moment.

"Look after Joe," Colette said quietly. She didn't say anything else, but her eyes pointed. Following them, Ren saw Mariel hushing the crying girl. She put an arm around Colette and together, they enveloped the rest of the group. Joe, stuck in the center, wiped away the tears and the solemnity and growled softly.

"Oh my god, I'm fine! Get off me!" She tried to sound offended, but couldn't hold in the laughter trickling through her words.

Ren pulled Colette and Mariel closer, tightening the circle around Joe again. She looked between them, smiling wide.

"Do you think she's okay?" Colette smiled back.

"I don't know; she could be in denial."

"Maybe we should keep it up for a while longer."

Mariel laughed, kissing Colette on the cheek. She turned, putting her arms around Ren and kissed her as well, folding her into a hug. The warmth burned from inside her and she felt the tears come unbidden.

"We'll be back before you have a chance to miss us," Mariel smiled, but hesitated.

Ren raised an eyebrow, but the moment was gone. Mariel squeezed her again, then, turned her attention to breaking up the huddle. "Good night, ladies."

Joe put her arm around Ren, who leaned hard against her sister to keep them both from pitching over.

"Come on, lush, I'll help you find your room," Joe laughed, both of them taking it slow as they moved to the stairs.

"Listen, wino," Ren countered as they both put an arm around each other, and each an arm on the railing. "Without me, you'd already be on the floor."

Together, they trudged, one step at a time, retorts being shuffled back and forth with the same amount of ferocity as their conquest of the staircase.

"You'd never have gotten this far without my help." Joe tried to jab a ticklish spot in Ren's side, disturbing the sleepy equilibrium they shared. Together, they paused to grip the railing harder and make sure their feet were still beneath them.

Ren snickered. "My room is first, so we'll see how far you can get on your own."

Once they had made it to Ren's room, they had all but won. Ren leaned into the dark, knowing her bed would catch her, and indeed it did. She also dragged Joe with her, who pitched forward into the darkness with a sense of panic and hoped for the best. When she found herself safely cradled by the overstuffed duvet somewhere in the darkness, she let her worries slip to the floor and hoped Ren didn't kick in her sleep.

SEVEN

In the night, there was a sound that crawled along the walls of the room. A long, rasping hiss seemed to climb from the dark recesses under the bed, up to the hidden corners of the ceiling before it finished. Ren heard it through dreaming senses. When she heard it again, her eyes opened wide, investigating – not that they did much good in the pitch-dark room. She listened to the noise slither around her a third time and reached out with her senses. She was face down on her bed, sleeping in her clothes on top of her plush comforter. She made a mental note that this wasn't an awful way to spend a night, minus the evil thing haunting her bedroom. If someone else were in here with her they could –

She reached across the bed, hoping to find that she had been carried to bed with something that would make a handy weapon. What she found was a hand. A hand that attached to an arm that attached to the ugly noise coming from Joe's lumbering breath.

Ren gritted her teeth, panic evaporating in the fire lit inside as she realized her panic was nothing more than her sister's disturbingly haunted snoring. She couldn't help herself. Reaching out, she pinched Joe's nostrils closed, snickering as the girl choked momentarily and coughed. As Joe reflexed, rising, Ren hit her with a pillow. Joe cried out, not fully awake and under attack.

"You could have told me you snore," Ren sighed, her senses returning to her as she collapsed back onto the bed.

"I do not snore," Joe's protest muffled by the pillow. She yawned. "Even if, you can sleep in your own bed."

"You are in my room!"

"Whatever."

Ren wanted to argue further, but she could already hear Joe drifting back to sleep. Ren laid back, her heart still trying to come back down to its resting beat. She knew staring up at the black nothing in front of her that she wouldn't be sleeping until the adrenaline finished worming through her system.

Maybe a cup of tea will help. And a book.

She sat up slowly, easing off the bed. She was tired, but she didn't feel any of the effects she expected to after the night they had all had.

Let's count ourselves lucky and not push that little bonus too often.

She eased open the door and slipped out, fingers gliding along the railing as she walked toward the stairs. Looking down, she was surprised to see a light cutting across the room. One thin beam traced along the floor up to the door of Mariel's office, the door closed all but a crack. She wandered across to the kitchen, moving quietly. Whatever Mariel found so important to be up at this hour, Ren didn't want to interrupt her just yet. She moved as silently as possible, transferring the kettle to the stove, heating the water to a boil without the whistle in place. While the water began to roil, she prepared the tea tray. The dark was easier to work with here, soft blue light glowing through the windows allowing her to see enough to work by. She transferred the kettle to the serving tray and carried the whole set across the common room in the dark, back to the sliver of light beaming from Mariel's office. She approached the door and braced one knuckle, rapping twice, soft but firm and stood quietly in the dark.

She heard a shuffle and the door opened quietly to a curious face. Mariel's lips parted in a warm smile the moment she opened the door.

"I couldn't sleep," Ren spoke in a whisper. "And I thought you could use a break."

Mariel stepped out of the way, welcoming her into the cramped office. No, cramped wasn't right. There was plenty of room to move, but every available surface was dedicated to books and instruments and artifacts, rested upon old wood surfaces and stacked on each other. The room adhered to a completely different set of rules than the rest of the house. Strange books from all eras, in many languages. Intricate devices that Ren knew with just a look she had better not touch. Piles of pages and stones and coins. Unlike the other rooms and boxes and showcases; there was no central theme in this room. It seemed to be a collection of oddities that Mariel surrounded herself with.

Then the light flicked on in Ren's head: Mariel was the connection. This was her personal collection.

Mariel pulled a flat drawer from her desk, providing a place for the serving tray. Ren set it down, pouring two cups of steaming water. She took a teabag with her cup and sat down at the other side of the desk, exhaling across the lip of the cup, watching steam dance and dissipate into the room.

Mariel raised her cup. "Fortune is certainly in my favor tonight. Thank you." Ren raised her cup in reply.

"What do you mean?" She looked across the desk. Whether it was the light or the hour, Mariel did not look like her usual self. She looked weary, like her years were catching up to her tonight. Ren swallowed, that was a lot of time to weigh on a person all at once.

Mariel looked down, passing a page across the desk. Ren saw the refined, flowing script on the page, then she saw her own name.

"I have been sitting down here trying to leave you with some sort of explanation for our departure. Lord knows you deserve something."

"Mariel, I really don't. I —"

Mariel cut her off. She set her cup down. "You do. You should at least understand the responsibility we are leaving you with."

Ren sat back. She looked at the page again, and then back to Mariel. "Okay."

Mariel adjusted herself, taking a breath.

"I am not going to tell you why we are going. Some things are not your concern." She gauged Ren's reaction. The girl was trying to understand without looking too shaken. "For now." She added, hoping it would placate Ren's worries.

"What I do need to tell you, what you need to understand, is exactly what you are being entrusted with here." She stood and turned to the shelves behind her. Ren could see her lingering on various objects, then moving to the next. "In the main rooms, we showcase a particular collection, because we can afford to. The grants that help sustain us make that collection vital, both in the caretaking and continued expansion. But there are far more interesting objects that do not fit with our showcase." She smiled as she turned around and flipped a coin onto the table. It landed with a ringing thud on the desk, the weight obvious in the sound. Ren picked up the coin and examined it. The side she could see was a roman numeral circled by laurels. On the opposite face, was a detailed picture of –

She gasped and almost dropped the coin in surprise. Mariel chuckled as Ren looked again. She blinked, turning the coin over again. Her eyes were not mistaken: there was a depiction of a couple sharing an intimate, if not lewd, moment on the flipside of the coin. She reached out, returning it to Mariel.

"They have the internet for that sort of thing now, you know," Ren couldn't help but make faces; it was a shock, especially for this hour.

"It is called a spintria," Mariel flipped it over in her fingers. "Roman. First century."

She watched Ren's mouth repeat the words soundlessly. She could almost see the wheels start working. "Yes, it is worth quite a bit, but probably not as much as you would think. I will not bother you with a history lesson tonight, but it is an example. There are many valuable objects in this house." Her gaze wandered the room, then, settled on Ren.

"Guard them. Care for them. But remember: None of this is worth putting yourself at risk."

Ren nodded but the gears were still turning. She had been training. She was getting pretty good at both hand to hand and swordplay – with a wooden sword, but it was close to the same thing, right? Surely, she could defend Delaney house if it came down to it.

Mariel had been raising her cup to sip. She lowered it and cut Ren off with a single glance.

"Do not forget, Ren: There are no guarantees on the second chance we have been given." She shook her head. "Nothing in this house is worth your life."

"Maybe not nothing," Ren smiled. "*You* risked a lot to bring me here."

"Touché," Mariel sipped her tea. "She plays tough, but she's a delicate soul. Look after her." There was no acknowledgement to whom she was referring. Ren waited, watching Mariel enjoy her tea without anything further.

"Joe?" She sat up a little. "She was a little blubbery, but I think the wine had a lot to do with that."

Mariel nodded, putting her cup down again. She didn't look at Ren and for a moment, it appeared she was done with the discussion.

"She would not tell you this herself. Josephine is very self-conscious of her past and would rather you accept her for the person she is becoming – without the burden she carries with her."

Ren paused again, confused. This all seemed to be coming out of nowhere. "We are talking about the same Joe, right?"

"Yes, the wonderful girl who I presume is passed out upstairs. The one with the good heart and the strong spirit." To Ren, it felt like the room darkened as Mariel leaned toward the desk, looking Ren in the eye. "Like the rest of us, that bright-eyed girl comes with a past much darker than her future."

"Josephine was orphaned very young. No one else in her family came to collect her, and she entered the foster care system." Ren continued to listen, feeling like they were discussing a different Joe – but Mariel was right, each of them had come here from some ugly end. She hated to think that her past, dark as it was, might have been the brightest of them. "Regardless of what the system reported, she grew up alone. She was not much more than a statistic to the courts, a paycheck to her caretakers."

Ren cradled her cup close, as if the warmth radiating from the tea might warm the cold spot growing in her heart as she listened.

"She was a mixed up young girl who grew into a mixed up and angry young woman. Her pain turned inward and she began to lash out at herself." Mariel found a spot on the wall to focus on, the soft glow in the room betraying her composure as the light glinting off waiting tears. "When Josephine hurts, she hurts herself. At the beginning, it was hard to watch. We kept her close and worked with her and slowly, she began to adjust. She accepted us and started to trust us as a family. But her first life…"

Ren held the tissue box out to Mariel who could barely thank her, the words coming out weak and broken, wet with tears. Ren held it in as best she could. It wasn't that she didn't feel every ounce of anguish that Mariel did, but she didn't want to miss a word. She didn't want these words to ever have to be repeated again.

Mariel took another minute to compose herself, breathing deeply, each breath growing steadier upon exhale. Finally, she looked up again.

"She spiraled for a long time, distracting herself from the misery around her by cutting herself. She was convinced that it made her strong; that the pain was the only thing in her life she could count on. But she could not take it any longer." Mariel paused, her mouth quivering as she tried to finish. "She gave in. She —"

Ren held out an open palm, she couldn't trust her words to do their part just now. She felt a small relief when Mariel stopped, the story ended. Ren could only stare, her surroundings a watery blur behind the tears. She couldn't even imagine the misery and loneliness that Joe must have felt to take such drastic actions. Ren had lost her mother, ostracized herself, and somehow still managed to rise up and return to life in general. She couldn't fathom the agony required for her to surrender her life. Her heart swelled again and she felt her face flush. Words could not be trusted for the moment; they'd only lead to more tears.

"It was only twenty years ago. I know that is literally a lifetime ago for you, but for her, it is still very fresh."

The weight of the moment hung thick in the air. She wasn't sure if she should inquire further or just agree. Instead, Ren let the moment linger; they finished their tea in silence. Ren returned her cup to the serving tray and broke the still of the room. She leaned across, putting a hand over Mariel's.

"I'll look after her. She'll be my top priority." Mariel put another hand over Ren's, pressing as she smiled. "But make sure you and Colette come back to us quick. Two girls, alone in a house like this. We'll probably spend all your spintria on booze and have wild parties every night."

Mariel stood, laughing softly and hugged Ren. "Good luck. Spintria are tokens for Roman brothels." She laughed louder as she felt Ren shudder. "Good night, my dear."

* * * *

By the time Ren and Joe had dragged

themselves out of bed, Mariel and Colette were already gone. Ren noticed their absence almost immediately. There was a warmth gone from the rooms. Not physical warmth, but a psychological one.

A sensation she hadn't actually been aware of until it was taken away. It didn't feel like home anymore. But more than the change in the house, there was a change in Joe. She moved and responded with a malaise Ren could not have anticipated. She dragged through the morning as if hung over, but Ren was almost positive that wasn't the case.

Separation anxiety, she frowned. *Mom and big sis are off on a trip and you got stuck with the babysitter.*

She sat across from Joe, watching her nibble at the edges of a pop tart. She hadn't lifted her eyes from their due-south orientation since she'd gotten on her feet. She made eye contact with Ren once, when she first opened her eyes. That was an hour ago.

Ren poured a cup of coffee and smiled.

"So what should we do with our first day of freedom?"

Joe shrugged, not looking up.

"We could go shopping. Get matching tattoos. Adopt a puppy!"

Again, Joe only shrugged. Ren was disappointed; she was only half kidding about the matching tattoo idea. She dragged her cup with her, half turning from the table where her little black raincloud continued to scratch away at her breakfast with record shattering apathy.

"If you change your mind, come find me. We'll have an adventure." She tried not to sound desperate as she said it, but felt herself suppress a scream as Joe shrugged again. She left the room and moved out to a chair in the common room, throwing a leg up over one arm and finding an awkward looking position that was perfectly comfortable for reading.

Ren found that while contortionist positions seemed to help her focus on the relaxing art of reading, the sudden apathy in her friend and roommate did the exact opposite. She abandoned the book to the coffee table and moved to the upstairs rooms where she could lose herself in the history contained there and, perhaps, accidentally get some work done in the process.

She had barely opened the door when she

staggered. A memory had been waiting for her to return to this room and now that she had, it jumped at her like an untrained puppy, yipping the same rhythmic sound in her brain over and over.

The journal! The journal! The journal!

She moved immediately to the box, opening it to see if anything had been moved or replaced since her last visit. William Delaney's journal was still missing. This meant that the game was still afoot, or it really had been moved with purpose. She pondered this as she moved to the next container, carrying it to the table and setting it down for examination.

* * * *

Downstairs, a little black raincloud continued to mope at the kitchen table. She wasn't at all interested in eating, but was so lost in thought that her motor skills continued without her insistence. She was tired, but it was a mental exhaustion. The fact that she was up most of the night was not nearly as taxing as the notion that she had spent that conscious time fuming.

She had woken when Ren attacked her, but not completely. Part of her returned to sleep quickly, but part of her remained awake and alert; poking at her brain and asking the kind of questions that were certain to get it up and moving.

What time is it? Where is Ren going in the dark? What if monsters eat her?

Joe sat up. It wasn't a rational collection of thoughts, but what set of questions from a sleeping brain were? Regardless, she was up and at least conscious, if not yet alert. She waited. Perhaps Ren had just gone to the bathroom – or for a drink. It seemed a logical conclusion, so she lay back down. She did not sleep. Instead, her brain conjured a multitude of other things that Ren could be doing – or suffering – somewhere outside the bedroom. She took a deep breath, trying to regain calm, and waited. The minutes stretched into hours – or did they? Time was such a funny thing. Unless you were actually aware of its passage, you had no idea how long it had been. Even if you were aware, sometimes it could still trick you. Joe got up. She could laugh off her childish paranoia later – in the daylight.

She crept quietly out of the room, wanting not to wake anyone else. Over the railing to the stairs, she saw the light creeping out of Mariel's office and the questions started again, full force.

What is she doing? What is so pressing it can't wait till morning? What if she's stealing? Why wouldn't she wait till Mariel left?

Joe moved down the stairs and across the common room evenly and quietly. She crept to the door, ready to have at least her more reasonable curiosities answered, but stopped before she got to the door.

There were two voices and they were discussing *her*.

Joe felt her throat tighten and her face flush. Were they worried what she might do without anyone watching her? After all these years, she was still the child? After all she had done to prove herself to her sisters – that she was safe and sane – they still treated her like the baby – even with a fledgling sister right under the same roof! Her jaw set and she glared at – through – the door for a long while, then, turned toward the stairs.

She would have it out with Ren in the

morning, after Mariel and Colette had gone.

She would voice her frustrations and pull rank if she had to. It was her right as the older sister.

She moved back up the stairs, disappearing into the dark of Ren's room just as the door opened downstairs, scattering light everywhere. Quietly, she closed the door and tried to recall her sleeping position as she lay back down. Realizing too late, she should have just gone to her room. But the door was already opening in the dark and Joe instinctively froze. Ren was obviously ready to go back to sleep as she trudged into the room, her hands padding around, seeking out Joe's position before collapsing. The hands found her, gently tracing until they located her face. Ren leaned forward, kissing her sister on the forehead before collapsing on the other side of the bed.

To anyone else, this would have been a loving gesture. But in the dark, Joe only glared, the kiss feeling more like a slap in the face.

She carried this burning resentment with her into the morning, where it festered. She could hear what sounded like confusion in Ren's voice

– as if she didn't know what she'd done – and pushed it aside. There would be plenty of time to explain it to her, when Joe finally pushed down enough of the anger to form words.

* * * *

When Ren finally closed the box, fatigue settled immediately behind her eyes. She had no idea how long she had been pouring over the objects in this treasure trove, but her stomach informed her that too many hours had come and gone since she last sought sustenance. She closed her eyes and massaged the bridge of her nose, willing the raw exhaustion from her brain. She had stared too intently at the objects for far too long. A moment passed while Ren worried about causing herself nearsightedness. Could that even happen? She didn't know, but she certainly didn't want to spend an eternity with failing eyesight.

She grabbed the empty coffee cup off the desk and took it with her, stumbling dreamily into the hall. The rays of sunlight that had stretched across the floor were no longer present. Currently, they rested upon the windowsill, which told Ren she had definitely missed lunchtime.

Strolling into the empty kitchen, she noticed that Joe's plate was still on the table. Not only that, but her pop tart was still sitting, mostly uneaten, on the plate. She raised an eyebrow, but shrugged it away. Maybe Joe was hung-over after all.

Ren rummaged through the fridge, grabbing at jars of this and bottles of that. Stuffing them into the crook of one arm, she piled odds and ends on top, intent on making one trip from fridge to counter. Laziness sometimes required an intense amount of will and intent, making her wonder why lazy people considered themselves lazy at all.

Because if you didn't have to, you definitely wouldn't. She nodded in agreement.

It's true that, sometimes, Ren could be lazy. Pretending she didn't hear the phone so she didn't have to answer it. Being slower to react so she didn't get stuck on certain chores. Barely making an effort to get out of bed on days off. Ren could be lazy like a champ. But most of the time, she was efficient to a fault.

She smiled satisfactorily at her haul. Not an

ingredient missed. It was going to be a good day for sandwiches. She piled on the meats and cheeses, adding some lettuce and tomato, watching it teeter like a jenga tower while she considered the best tactic for delivering this mammoth of a sandwich to its final resting place.

She twisted the bread bag closed and turned, spying the orphaned pop tart on the table.

It was only a momentary pause, but to the casual observer, Ren continued her twirl, turning right back to the counter where she set to work building a second towering delight. For a moment, she considered that Joe might not be as hungry as she was, but decided too much was always better than not enough.

With a plate in each hand and a soda can stuffed precariously into each pocket, she made her way up the stairs and to Joe's door, where she announced her presence to the obviously-unimpressed wooden surface.

"Knock knock."

There was no answer. Not even the telltale rustle of sheets or the squeak of bedsprings that usually accompanies someone rising up in reaction. Ren tossed her hair back and forth as she debated. Joe could be sleeping off whatever had been dragging her down earlier, or she could be ignoring the door. This left Ren with the choice of interrupting a potentially necessary nap or coming back later when it was more convenient.

Ren smiled and banged the side of the plate against the door, listening to it thunk deep and hollow on the other side.

"Room service! Would ze young miss like her pillows fluffed?" She clamped her lips shut between her teeth, but the words had already come out. She felt a tinge of red spreading across her cheeks. "Um, that sounded a lot worse than I meant it."

And still, there was no reaction. Not a laugh or a squeak or anything. If she'd actually left, she'd left no message, which was actually worse than ignoring Ren across the expanse of a bedroom door. This might be moody, but that would be plain rude.

Her ears perked and her eyes widened, as if letting more light in would improve her ability to see through wood. There had been a squeak, a definite cringe of protest from bedsprings. She pressed her face against the wood, lips tight to the panel before her.

"I know you're in there." Her accusing tone, combined with the complication of speaking against the door turned her words into a low drone the likes of which would have impressed any second rate mummy in history.

"Little pig, little pig, let me in!" She banged the plates against the door for emphasis, making a racket that almost hindered her words. At this point, she didn't care; she just wanted to be acknowledged. "Or I'll huff and I'll puff –"

The door flew open, clattering against the wall. Startled, Ren's words caught in her throat and she stumbled back a little. Joe stood glaring on the other side of the threshold. It took a moment, but Ren collected herself and smiled, holding out a plate.

"I made you a sandwich. I thought you might be hungry."

After I saw your breakfast still on the table. She meant to finish, but Joe turned without a twitch of reaction and walked back to the bed where she slumped back onto it.

Ren stepped into the room, setting the plates

on top of the dresser. She looked at Joe, then around the room. It wasn't her first time in Joe's room, she'd been here countless times but something was different. The shades were drawn, making the burgundy walls seem much more oppressive. The whole room felt claustrophobic and slightly threatening.

It was likely she was reading too much into the moment. She could tell something was bothering Joe, and that something was being directed at her.

"Looks like I'm not the huffy one." Ren smiled as she turned to the dark shape on the bed, arms crossed and face impassive. "Something you want to talk about?"

"Don't even."

Anywhere else in the house and she might have missed it. But here, the dark swallowed her need to see. The silence of the room made every sound important, her ears picked up those two small words and every bit of anger that was carried on the quiet breath that spoke them.

"Did I," Ren didn't want to finish the question, she felt very small and selfish all of the sudden. "...do something?"

"Did you?" She sat bolt upright, her face still a mask but fire burning in her eyes as she glared at Ren. "Why bother asking? You don't actually care."

"What are you –" Ren took a step back, her hand raising and pressing to her chest. It was an instinctive motion. The words made her heart hurt. Not the physical, beating one, but the one where love resided. She'd always thought of it as symbolic, the heart, until her mother died. She felt it then, as she felt it now, like a stake driven deep into a muscle tied to her life force. It seemed the only time she was aware of her heart was when it hurt like this.

"How can you say that, Joe? I thought we –"

"I thought we did too." Her dark voice choked for a second. "I heard you talking with Mariel last night." One swift motion and she was on her feet. She was scorn and fury, and somewhere within, sadness. Even in the minimal light of the room, Ren could see the tears that rimmed the girl's eyes.

"Joe, shh," She took a step closer, trying to recall exactly what they'd discussed over tea, what might have been misrepresented. "Whatever you heard –"

"She said I was weak! And you said you'd take charge." She stomped in place, her lip quivering. "I am not weak! I am just as strong as the rest of you!" Trembling fingers dipped into her pocket, withdrawing a pocketknife. The blade glinted like the tears in Joe's eyes and Ren felt another shot of pain through her symbolic heart.

"Joe, don't. You don't have to prove anything."

"You're going to keep talking behind my back until I do." She winced as the blade bit into the flesh. "I am stronger than the pain."

The tears were streaming now, from both sets of eyes in the room, both sets focused on the knife and the blood. Ren stepped forward and placed a gentle hand on Joe's, enveloping and pulling the knife away from her wounded flesh. Their eyes met and for a moment, both saw shame reflected in the other's gaze.

"I am so sorry." Ren said through her own quivering lips. "I just wanted to keep you safe. I..."

The rest of the words she meant to say were lost in a cascade of tears as she looked down at the wounded arm. Ren took the hand and pulled it close, tugging at her shirt to wrap loose fabric around the bloody wound. The gesture was desperate and clearly not thought out, but she didn't know what else to do. Her brain screamed for her body to act, and so she did. She tried to put pressure on, but only served to smear the blood around, making a bigger mess of Joe's arm and her shirt. Somewhere in the chaos, the knife thudded to the carpet and Joe's free hand tried to calm the commotion.

"It's alright. It stops after a while." She spoke through tears and shuddering breath.

"I'm sorry." They both said it at the same time, responding with half-smiles and happy tears as Ren pulled Joe into a crushing hug. Her only response was to hug back.

"Let's never fight again. Please." Joe spoke, shame still riding on her words.

"Never. I promise." Ren held her tighter.

"Don't –" Joe tried to protest. "I'm bleeding all over you."

"Shut your stupid face and hug me."

EIGHT

True to Joe's statement, the bleeding stopped before long. What did get out seemed to be everywhere. In her panic to stop the bleeding, Ren had transferred the mess to both sides of her t-shirt, her skin, all over her arms, and under her fingernails. When she thought she had wiped away the whole mess, she would find a spot overlooked. Her moment of terror was all but evaporated in the frustration with getting clean. Joe didn't seem to have any trouble cleaning up, which only furthered her annoyance.

"It's like glitter! It's worse! Glitter doesn't spread nearly as much – or as far!"

Ren wandered back into Joe's room, dressed

in a new outfit and almost certain that a shower wouldn't have been such an extreme response as she originally thought.

"So, the defining aspect of my blood being worse than glitter is its viscosity?" Joe made a skeptical frown back at Ren as she finished dressing the wound. She had also changed, but didn't point out that it was as much to shed the feelings from earlier as it was to rid herself of the soiled fabric. "Perhaps I should have all this pesky blood replaced with glitter, so as not to annoy you so much next time."

Ren clucked her tongue. "You wouldn't survive. You'd be hunted by strippers and ravers, like hungry vampires after your precious life-giving glitter."

The corners of Joe's frown deepened, her eyes glaring slightly.

"Let's never talk about that again. It sounds like an awful way to go."

They had decided that the first order of business was to get out of the house. There was going to be plenty of time to be cooped up later. She wanted Joe away from any reminders for the time being. Not that she was worried about a repeat of the earlier turmoil, but she could see the self-consciousness in Joe's eyes now. She needed to get Joe out of her head, and she needed the same for herself as well. In the back of her mind, Ren was still thinking about the missing journal. She was certain that the old book would be scratching at the back of her brain until she solved the mystery; she could only hope it would happen quickly – but later. Today, they had decided on a different sort of adventure – and perhaps some consumer therapy.

Ren's feet bounded down the steps and she stopped in a patch of sun. Her eyes closed as she arched her back, spreading her arms out instinctively. Whether she was blossoming in the light, or planning to float off the earth, she didn't care. The air smelled of life and the sun poured warmth and happiness into her heart and soul. She breathed deep and held onto it, finally exhaling in a euphoric rush.

Joe tried to prod her along, but Ren grabbed her hand and held it.

"Stop. Smell the roses, Joe."

"There are no roses."

"Humor me. It's something my mother used

to say."

"Your mother used to call you Joe?"

"I'm not speaking to you again until you do this. Right now; with me." She closed her eyes again and let her senses drift outward. She heard the distant traffic, the birds and the light breeze in the trees around them, faint voices. She could feel life going on around them and she wanted to savor this moment.

This moment that almost wasn't, she reminded herself.

"You realize that there will be other days like this, right?" She heard Joe speak from the other side of her bliss.

"Mom also used to say, 'every day is a gift, Florence. Don't waste it'."

Somewhere in those words, Joe realized just how right Ren was. How many days had she let slip by unappreciated since her new life started? How often did she take it all for granted so easily? When she woke this morning, the hope and happiness were gone from the world. Now, they had returned and she responded to it with sarcasm. She tried to shake off the negativity and smile as she looked over at this purple-haired sunflower; a small but insistent smile on her face as she stared, eyes closed into the sunshine. She didn't know if this was the reason that Mariel left her in charge, but this was definitely the reason Joe was going to accept. Ren had things she could teach Joe, if she was willing to listen, to learn. Things Ren might not even be aware she was teaching.

Joe closed her eyes and allowed herself to feel the sunshine. She wondered how she couldn't feel it like this the whole time. She could almost see herself awash in the golden sunlight, warm and content. More instinct than imitation, her arms spread from her sides, and Joe allowed herself to blossom in the sun.

In three and a half blocks the quiet serenity of their peaceful, anonymous neighborhood had erupted into bustling chaos. Everywhere, people hurried; they were meandering in and out of storefronts, examining produce sold from open car trunks and truck beds, finding places to congregate. The air smelled of flowers and cookouts; Ren's mouth began to water, even though she had only finished lunch a short time ago. They strolled the sidewalk, matching pace with wandering shoppers ahead of them. There were galleries and specialty shops and corner markets, each one embracing a niche of their own.

Joe took Ren by the elbow and led her out of the bright sun, into a small doorway. Her eyes adjusted, spying a long wooden counter topped in glass, jewelry and ornamentals displayed under the protective surface. The wall behind the counter was a display of its own. The ends were faced in large glass door, displaying expensive looking silver and crystal within. Between the large glass cases was a wall of drawers, smaller ones at eye level, and methodically growing in size as they neared the floor. Every bit of wood was meticulously carved and well maintained. The cabinetry reminded her of the old general stores, where you could buy all your supplies in one place.

Or an apothecary. She smiled using the word, and wished she'd said it out loud. She loved to flex her vocabulary; words needed to be remembered too, lest they be forgotten entirely.

The store had since been replaced by a boutique. Joe was gravitating to a series of bright colors and flowy fabrics in the back corner. Ren giggled softly as she heard Joe exclaimed out loud, almost trancelike as she pulled one off the wall.

"Ren, look at it!" She held it up to herself, smoothing it down her body as Ren navigated the obstacles, nodding.

"I said: Look at it."

"I am."

"Yes, but not appreciatively."

"It's very... unique."

"That's not appreciative either."

Joe was not mistaken in her interpretation. She spun toward the mirror, smoothing it down her again. It was a tunic dress, with a low V-cut on the front and back. There was almost nothing to the dress; it was a series of panels sewn together, yet it had a certain charm to its simplicity. What Ren couldn't bring herself to appreciate was the pattern stamped upon the fabric: teal, patterned in pink, green and purple. She wanted to believe it was a repeating flower pattern, but looking too closely gave her a slight sensation of vertigo.

"Tunic dresses just aren't my thing."

There was a pause while Joe considered her, then rolled her eyes and regarded her reflection again.

"I guess I don't have to worry about you trying to borrow it then."

Ren smirked. "You definitely don't have to worry about that."

The day rolled along, and each hour gave way to the next, the only real sense of time passing was a growing pang of hunger. Solidly burdened with successful purchases, Ren led them to one of the food trucks at the end of the street, following the scent of barbeque like a bloodhound. She navigated the waning crowd and found herself a place in queue, bouncing on the balls of her feet as she inhaled deeply. Joe watched her with a mixture of scientific curiosity and amusement.

"You're a strange person, you know that?"

Ren smiled, continuing to bounce as the line ticked down to her turn.

"There's nothing wrong with a healthy appreciation for food."

"*Children* are less excited about *ice cream*."

Her eyes lit up. "We should get ice cream

after this!"

"There's no hope for you."

"We all have our burdens. Yours is a tunic dress."

"There's nothing wrong with my dress."

Ren smiled, stepping up to the window and doing her best to rid them of as much slow-cooked meat as she could reasonably handle. They found an unoccupied park bench and built a makeshift fortification of their purchases, defending themselves as they shared the meal. The art of conversation had given way to primitive communication in a series of grunts and appreciative moans.

It had become apparent that closing time was carrying on all around them. The sun was still up, but had begun to disappear behind the taller buildings in the old district.

Theirs was the only occupied bench in sight, most cars had disappeared from the street and only a handful of people were still travelling the sidewalks.

The street was so quiet and peaceful as they ate, Ren almost never noticed their audience. After a few appreciative bites, she finally opened her eyes, seeing the woman from across the street. She was hunched over, her fingers a bony claw around the handle of her cane. Her face seemed slack and unresponsive; she could have been sleeping on her feet, for all Ren knew. It was more that she felt the gaze than actually saw it. It was not a pleasant sensation, either. It made her lose her appetite.

"What's wrong?" Joe looked up, working the words around a bite of pork.

She nodded her head in the direction of the old woman, taking another bite of her sandwich. She would not let Eunice Abernathy ruin her barbeque.

"I don't like her. She just keeps staring."

"Maybe she's having a senior moment and forgot where she parked."

"Maybe she's having a Hannibal Lecter moment."

"Oh come on, she's like eighty."

"Aren't you the one that accused her of witchcraft?"

Joe balked, not certain if she had actually said such a thing, even though it did sound like her. Ren made grabbing claw motions with her greasy fingers, reaching out slowly toward Joe.

"My, aren't you a little morsel," Joe tried to bat the hands away, as Ren rasped out a witchy cackle. "Oh, give Jenny Greenteeth a taste." She smacked her lips loudly, and Joe slapped her hand away.

"Never use that voice again, that's creepy."

"Oh and that isn't?" She gestured with her eyes at the old woman on the opposing sidewalk.

"It's not like she's hurting anyone," Joe turned and gestured to the place where Eunice Abernathy had been standing. "She's not even there anymore, so you can quit your crying."

"I wasn't crying."

"You were a little."

Ren bent her fingers at ugly angles and hunched as she stood. "Jenny Greenteeth wants a hug."

Joe stepped around the park bench, trying to keep it between them.

"Get away!"

"Delicious little morsel."

"Stop it!"

Joe swung around the bench and grabbed her bags, stumbling backward for a moment before turning and trotting to the end of the block. Ren laughed, picking up her bags and tossed the remains of their meal away. She tried to contain her laughter as she walked to the corner Joe waited at. Joe pointed threateningly at her, backing up even more.

"No more Jenny Greenteeth! It's creepy."

Ren tried to reply in her witch voice, but she was laughing too hard to continue.

The pair wandered back to the house, their laughter coming without prompting or reason; the telltale sign of an enjoyable if not exhausting day. By the end of the jaunt, both were dragging their heels, heads bobbing as they passed through deepening shadows.

The house was a welcome sight. It meant refuge after their long adventure. Ren had never wanted a long relaxing bath so much in her life. Joe grabbed her wrist and Ren put her other hand on it. They were both going to sleep very well tonight.

Joe squeezed and tugged Ren's arm, waking Ren from her daze. Joe had stopped altogether. She was eyeing the house suspiciously. Ren looked between the house and her sister once, twice, and on the third time, it clicked. A window in the main room was open. It was slight. No one else would have noticed, but Delaneys agonize over the details.

They stared at the window in the failing light. Was it a burglar? Were they still in the house? Minutes passed in the dark without a sound or movement. Finally, Ren moved.

Joe gasped, almost cried out. She covered Joe's mouth quickly, hoping she caught the sound in time. Ren whispered as she carefully released Joe.

"I'm going to slip in the back. Watch the front."

Joe nodded. "Wait. What if they come out?"

"Take them out."

"Kill them?"

"Try to tackle them first."

She felt Joe nod slowly again and started across the lawn, instinctively travelling on the balls of her feet.

She slipped into the servant entrance without a sound. It was easy when you had keys and oiled hinges. She moved into the common room, moving slowly, each step deliberate and silent.

She heard a quiet sound and froze. She waited, trying not to breathe – she heard it again, on the other side of the main door. Whoever it was, they were still keeping themselves busy in the front rooms. She imagined cat burglars putting their grimy hands all over her finely polished silver and felt a flush of anger in her cheeks. The likelihood that they were wearing gloves was not a consolation.

Though she wanted to rush, she continued to stealth her way across the room toward the door. She had no idea what to expect. No one had warned her what to do in the event of a break in. She wondered if they'd ever had to worry about break-ins before.

The house itself was well built and structurally secure. A locked window should have meant a secure window. Not only was the house usually quite secure, but also its contents were a treasure anyone could visit. The collection was highly valued, but not monetarily.

No thief was going to get very far with any of William Delaney's personal effects, especially once the word got out.

She focused on silent movement as she

reached the door. The dead bolt was still turned to the locked position. No one had come this far. That was at least good news. She closed her eyes and tried to will the dead bolt to move quietly, silently. She knew it wouldn't, so she tried to hope that whoever was on the other side of the door was not actually listening for trouble. She prayed for a burglar with an iPod.

Gently, one hand pushing while the other levered counter resistance, she turned the small lock slowly. It was agonizing. She didn't even know if the stupid thing was moving at all, then –

THUNK

The dead bolt slipped back into the door, safe and secure in the open position. It was as ominous a sound as the bump in the night she'd heard earlier.

She knew the person on the other side had heard it; there was no doubt. Slowly she turned the handle, ready to be rushed by a mysterious stranger. Little by little the door opened, Ren staying out of harm's way, not wanting to get hit with the door in the event of a powerful swing. The door opened wider, and no one came at her.

No one kicked in the door. She inhaled

deeply and breathed a sigh of relief before bracing herself for the worst as she stepped into the dark of the gallery.

She knew every step of the way, even in the dark, and tried to squint, looking for anything out of place. She moved evenly, face always forward. Her eyes, however, moved like crazy, looking at everything, trying to find that one element that didn't sit right. She tried to remain composed as she neared the window that had tipped them off.

She wanted a better look at the window from the inside, but she knew now wasn't the time. She kept walking, trying to reach the front door. The entire time, she expected to be assaulted, but none came. For her, this was a clue that their culprit was either a novice to crime, or to life itself. Again, she hoped her instincts were right.

A quick turn of her fingers confirmed that the front door was still locked tight. It was definitely the window. Someone had come in, which meant they could still be in here somewhere. With her. She took a deep breath and steadied her nerves. She was about to try something very dangerous. Every nerve in her body begged her not to, but deeper than that her sense of honor decided she needed to. She looked out into the room, scanning the darkness, studying the silhouettes. She traced along the wall and held her breath as she flicked on the first set of lights, watching the shadows jump and disappear in the lighted areas. In the others, they shifted, becoming brand new shapes.

One by one the switches came on, narrowing her search down to one lonely corner of the room. With each new light in the room, she grew anxious for something to happen, her certainty assuring her that it was about to, and certain where it was coming from as well.

Her fingers closed around the last switch and she paused. If someone was about to come at her, she knew she was not ready. She looked left, and right, her eyes falling on a turn of the century gentleman's cane. She remembered the card, "Hickory with silver handle, 1882." She grabbed it in one hand and flicked the switch to the on position.

Nothing happened.

She waited, expecting all hell to break loose, but nothing did. She tried to relax, but that wasn't going to happen. Ren believed someone was still in here, and she knew now that she had underestimated them. They were at least smart enough to keep their head down. It also meant they were waiting for an opportunity. One Ren wanted to assure would not happen.

She turned cautiously, looking into the meeting room. The room was sparsely decorated, mostly objects hung from the walls, and in the corners. There was nowhere for anyone to hide easily, unless they had crawled up into the fireplace. If they were willing to go that far to avoid discovery, she was curious enough to wait it out and see how they were going to get back out again.

She looked into the mess of showcases. It seemed like a logical and presentable organization until you hid a criminal somewhere in its midst. Then it suddenly became an overgrown jungle with pockets and hiding places galore. She inched forward, the cane gripped in both hands. Mariel had shown her plenty to defend herself against an unknown assailant, but she needed it to happen. Her nerves were fraying the longer this went on; too long without action and she might just collapse.

She stepped forward and moved around a cabinet, slinking low and pushing open its large bottom door. She prodded it open with the end of the cane. Empty. She reached down, grabbing the small handle with her fingers and pulled it back closed. Something darted out in her peripheral vision. All her brain identified was a hood and oversized clothing.

They were running away from her, not toward. Her throat went dry: they were headed for the common room. There was no way she was going to be able to find them if they slipped in there. Then she and Joe both would be in danger until it was over. She had to do something. She needed a moment to think – but there were no moments left to spend. Her instincts took over and before she knew it, she had already let the cane loose, turning end over end as it chased the intruder down the aisle, faster and more efficiently than she ever could have.

She heard the cane connect with the back of the hood: a loud, echoing crack. The figure crumpled and Ren shuddered at the awful sound. She wanted to feel bad, but at the same time, felt relief that the moment had passed and the crisis was over.

Unless there's more than one intruder. She hated her brain for having that thought, but she remained cautious just the same. Watching the collapsed figure, she moved to the window and waved Joe in.

The two girls stood over the crumpled heap, trying to decide what to do. Ren had already put Joe on alert as well; though they were both pretty sure this one was acting alone.

Black hoodie, gloves, and running pants. Definitely a thief.

Ren knelt next to the body, grabbing a shoulder. She heaved back, rolling the thief over onto its back. She corrected herself; it was definitely a he. She could see the broad chest and the firm jawline.

"Joe, get something to restrain him." Joe nodded and turned back to the common room.

She was going to suggest duct tape, but her voice abandoned her. All other thoughts that had been passing through her mind stopped dead in their tracks and gave their full attention to this moment.

Ren had one hand in a firm grip on the shoulder of the hoodie still, the other hand ready at a moment's notice to bring the cane up if she needed it, but she almost lost both as the hood fell back off his face.

He looked a few years younger than her, late teens at the oldest. He had short brown hair, cropped close in the military style. But it wasn't his hair that startled her – it was his face.

His brow was angled sharp as it curved toward the bridge of his nose. The nose itself was flat and wide and slightly rounded, but not like any other nose she had seen on a human face. His nostrils flared strangely from beneath the rim of his nose, rather than the sides. At first glance, his upper lip appeared to be swollen, but on a second inspection, it was split in two by an indentation and each half was more pronounced – like a cat's.

Exactly like a cat's.

His skin was covered in a short layer of fuzz – very much like fur – that gave his features a soft glow. She turned his head, almost expecting cat ears. To her disappointment, they were almost human. They were, however, pointed, set further back on his head, and curved deeper.

It didn't seem possible, but she was staring down into the face of a cat person. There was no other way to say it. She fought the magic of the moment and tried to pocket it away so she could gush later.

"What are you?" Her words were soft, stunned. Her brow creased with curiosity. He might have had the upper hand if he had rushed at her, not away. "What were you up to?" She looked around the room, from where he had been hiding, trying to will the answer to appear.

There was a gasp and a coo behind her as Joe returned with the tape, letting it fall to the carpet with a thud.

"He's beautiful. Is he–" Joe's eyes darted quickly between Ren and the collapsed figure.

"I don't know what he is. But he's definitely our burglar."

"*Cat* burglar." Joe snickered. Ren rolled her eyes, trying to hide her smile.

She gestured to his wrists and Joe grabbed them, Ren taking his ankles and they began to shuffle him out of the room. As they crossed the threshold, Ren eyed a chair to put him in. She gestured with her head and started shuffling in a new direction. They doubled up on the duct tape bindings, not certain how strong he was, or how capable. To the casual observer, their use of tape might seem excessive, but for them, it was best to be cautious. They were careful to keep the tape to clothed areas – it was bad enough pulling hairs when removing a bandage, she couldn't imagine the pain of taking the tape off his fur. When they finished, they eyed their handiwork and sat down, both curious about how long he'd be out.

As they waited, Joe cooed. "Do you think Mariel will let us keep him?"

NINE

Joe's fascination with their acquisition did not let up, even after two hours of silent slumber. She would find excuses to get up, studying him. She would watch carefully for minutes, making sure he was still unconscious, squinching up her face and tilting her head this way and that. She leaned in for better looks, ever closer. Carefully, cautiously. She moved like a lion tamer about to tempt fate by putting her head in the animal's mouth.

"You know, he's weird... but he's really cute." She looked to Ren for some sign of agreement. Ren could only raise an eyebrow over her book. "I don't mean like cute-cute, I mean adorable. Like I just want to pet his cute little nose."

"Relax, Joe."

"What?" She was much too close, even with his bindings. "Oh, right."

Joe went back to her spot on the couch, waiting impatiently. The knock to his skull was more severe than they presumed. Ren had leaned on the conservative side of estimates, but she had heard the sound. She knew how solid the contact was. She was hoping that she hadn't put him in a coma. She tried to remind herself that he had broken into their home; he had threatened their safety. It had been her only recourse. Ren felt bad for what she did, but mostly because Joe was right: he was adorable. It was hard to think that she had done harm to something – someone – so cute. She shook her head and tried to pry the thought loose. She wasn't going to be able to play tough if she kept thinking about his fuzzy little nose.

The room fell into a calm, the only real sound in the room being Joe's needles sliding against each other. It was a hobby Colette had started her on years ago, and she had found it both relaxing – as Colette had hoped – when she was doing well, and frustrating when she did badly. Keeping watch and knitting quickly without looking at her work was a recipe for ultimate disaster; as was apparent in her furrowed brow and gnashing teeth. Ren was trying to look calm. She continued to stare at the pages in front of her, occasionally turning to a new one, but she wasn't reading. She was trying to solve a riddle in her head. It seemed too coincidental, all these things happening at once.

First, Mariel and Colette leave on their trip. Then, she and Joe leave the house. Months without anything more volatile than a child putting chewing gum under the lid of an antique hope chest, now they were neck deep in a confrontation that would only get worse the moment he woke. She pursed her lips in frustration. Nothing was adding up yet; that meant that pieces of the puzzle were still missing.

Finally, after hours fearing the worst, he moaned slightly and his head lulled to the side. Joe perked up a bit too much in reaction to this. Ren snapped her book closed, hard, grabbing Joe's attention as Ren signaled her with one flash of a look. He raised his head, large wide eyes opened slowly, then blinked hard. They didn't reopen.

"No, no, no. Come on. It's about time you woke up, don't you think?" Joe looked back at her and Ren realized that her voice was not completely her own. She had stolen the note of authority Mariel usually spoke in. She had no desire to hurt him, but she would play tough as long as she was able. She needed answers and if it came down to intimidation, she might have to try it. She needed answers.

His eyes fluttered open again, and he gave the room a once-over with little recognition. His brain was still stunned. He blinked again, his eyes widening as his vision tracked back in the direction they had come. Though Ren tried to hold it in, they both gasped. His eyes were stunning. There was no sclera – no white to speak of at all – just a brilliant green and gold iris. The shimmering emerald pools each held one black oval stone deep within them. A stone that quickly disappeared into a thin black slit that sparked with fire and life as he came to.

He tried to move, whether to leap or charge, she wasn't sure, but the shoulders led and the legs followed, neither getting very far before his limbs met resistance. It didn't matter how quickly he had been forced back into his seat by gravity; they had both reacted. Ren had flinched and Joe leapt back. He tested his bindings twice more before he bared his teeth, glaring at them both under a heavy, angry brow.

"If you would just relax, we could get this all under way."

Ren played as cool as she could under the circumstances. She had to admit to herself that she didn't expect this much fight from him right away.

Someone really let the cat out of the bag on this one. She fought down a smile, but it still crept through. She'd have to find a time to work that in later.

He was panting, still trying to resist the bonds that contained him. He snapped his head back and forth between the two girls growling low and long.

"You're not going to get anything from me."

Ren shrugged. "Fine. You won't get anything from us either. You'll probably waste away to nothing in here, tied to that chair. How long do you think you can hold out?"

Joe leaned in; it was a good line to follow. "Better yet, how long do you think you can last before your butt goes numb? That's where the real torture begins."

Ren was not ready for the sudden tangent, but it appeared that he wasn't either. When she caught Joe's eye, she nodding, urging her on.

"That's one of those old church chairs that the altar boys sat in during mass. They're fine if you only need a minute or two to rest between sacraments, but murder on the glutes if you have to sit in it for any reasonable length of time. Sitting there is bad enough, but then you feel that nervous need to move, even just a shift of the weight." Ren was having a hard time keeping a straight face, but she had to admit, Joe was good. The burglar's face kept with her, his eyes only moving away for a moment, then snapping right back to her. She stumbled onto a very convincing argument. It was insane, but she was making it work. "Once it's in the muscles, the pain is in every movement. Good luck with that."

He shifted uncomfortably. The anger seemed to be gone from his eyes, but neither girl was about to let up their guard.

"Do you have a name? Something we can call you by at least?" Ren had accepted her role as 'good' cop, although she wasn't sure that Joe couldn't do both with this act.

"It's going to be weird trying to talk to you if we have to refer to you as 'Boy' or 'Guy' or 'Strange person that broke into our home.'"

He said nothing, his head bent at an uncomfortable looking angle as he stared downward.

They gestured back and forth over him, playing out a silent debate of what to do next. Ren realized she had no plan beyond where they already were. If he wasn't going to talk of his own accord, she couldn't see herself forcing him to do so. She could be forceful, but not torturous. Joe on the other hand, by the pantomimes she was making, was suggesting some creative forms of serious harm. Ren could only repeat the same motion over and over, meeting Joe's disappointed pout time and again.

They were so focused on interpreting each other's gestures; they almost missed the first step in the right direction.

It came in a small sigh and a long exhale, followed by a single word.

"Tau."

They looked back and forth, gesturing again.

Ren cleared her throat. "Well, that's about the last thing I was expecting." She scrambled for another question before he decided that way all the conversation he was in the mood for. "Um, how are you, Tau?"

He raised his head. His eyes sparkled, the anger rekindling a fire behind them.

"I am tied to an uncomfortable chair that you promise will only get worse. This is after an awful headache and a possible concussion. How do you think I am?"

Ren was taken back, feeling like she needed to go on the defensive. She paused and let the moment pass. He was playing with her. Maybe he was used to being in troubling situations. They were going to have to drive home the point that they would not be intimidated in their own home.

"If you hadn't broken in, this conversation wouldn't be taking place. At all. So don't blame us for your misfortune." Josephine intervened, showing an aggression that was not typically hers.

Ren let her have it. It was probably cathartic, and it seemed to be helping their cause as well. "Next question: what are you?"

He tried to glare, but resigned as he looked up at them.

"I am a Massay. My granddad used to say our people could be traced to ancient Egypt when Bast walked the Nile delta. She offered herself to men of superior power and skill, promising a family worthy of their superiority. She gave life to the Massay, her children."

Ren and Joe looked at each other.

"Bast. As in the Cat Goddess?"

He peered at Ren. "Does my face imply another deity?"

Joe jabbed Ren, laughing softly.

"Legend says that in the beginning, the Massay grew up side by side with their human brothers. But when the old ones were forgotten, prejudice began. My ancestors were treated like freaks, driven from their homes by angry mobs. First driven from Lower Egypt, then from Egypt completely. Many travelled south, deeper into Africa. The rest sought new lands, travelling into Asia. There, the remaining travelers parted ways.

Most headed further east, finally settling in China. The smallest group – the strongest of us – turned to the north and the west, eventually finding refuge in the forests of Eastern Europe."

"With the gypsies?" Ren's question was not necessarily meant for the open air, but it slipped out anyway. Tau shook his head with a small smile.

"The gypsies learned their way from us." The smile faded as he looked away. "It's hard to set up roots when your people are the source of the werewolf myth."

Ren and Joe looked at each other. It stood to reason: in the dark, glowing eyes and fangs could be anything, though eastern Europe is not necessarily known for large cats in their wilds.

The thought aside, they could only stare. His resignation had turned into full disclosure. They had no idea what to make of it. Even if he was making the whole thing up, he spoke with such certainty, such ease that it was clear he believed what he was saying.

"So, you're a… cat person." Joe curtailed.

"In layman's terms, sure. But I hardly consider myself anything as lowly and ordinary as a 'person.'"

"Fine. You're a being whose lineage traces back to a god. Sure. That doesn't explain why you broke into our home."

"I had no choice."

"There is always a choice." Ren spit the words, angered by his sudden case of pride.

"Right, but the alternative wasn't much of a choice, so here we are."

Ren feigned a pout. "It's always a bummer when the other option isn't grand larceny."

His eyes rimmed with red as he stared hard up at her. "Putting myself at risk here meant keeping my sister safe."

He cleared his throat and looked away as Ren's breath caught in her own. She looked to Joe instinctively, her hands clenched tightly together at the terrible thought.

"Panya was kidnapped and I was given specific instructions to steal a journal." Ren felt that pang again, the alarm ringing in her brain. "I will never see her again, unless I find that journal. I –" He coughed, his emotions getting the better of him. "I can't let her down."

Joe and Ren shared a look; Joe seemed

confused and concerned. Ren knew that now was not the time to divulge that she might know exactly what he was referring to. Could it be hidden away after all? As far as she was aware, there was only one that was not accounted for. It wasn't likely he was looking for any of the journals that were on display.

"Well, we can't just let you go." Ren ran a list of pros and cons in her head. She weighed the various factors of letting him go and was not really thrilled about any of the outcomes. "But we might be able to help." Joe and Tau both looked equally shocked. Joe's eyes only wanted to know whose brain was suddenly occupying the space in Ren's skull.

"First I'm beaten, now you want to help? Just tell me what you want."

"You broke in, we reacted. You're lucky she showed you mercy. You are in no position to be making demands." Joe was exercizing her bravado, and while Ren appreciated someone in her corner, filling the air while she stammered, it was really just dumb luck that she got the upper hand.

No one needs to know that part, though. Just like no

one needs to know there is a journal missing.

What had become of the journal in question? What did its absence mean? Why wasn't Mariel here to handle this one thing? How would she react to this? Had Mariel been keeping secrets? Ren clenched her fist and hoped that it was for her own protection. But she wasn't confident that was the case, not yet, and this wasn't the time for such small worries. There was a bigger issue at hand. Someone was after something in their house. Something important enough to already be missing. Where was it? Who moved it? And who is after it now?

Ren looked at Tau, studying his eyes. She took them in for a long time, wondering if they could be read the same way as the other eyes she'd seen through her life.

"Who told you about the journal?"

He shrugged and looked away. "I don't know. They wore hoods." Joe let out a skeptical sound. "If I knew, I'd tell you. What choice do I have at this point?" His eyes glistening as he tried to blink it away.

Ren motioned to Joe. She took her by the elbow and they stepped away from Tau, hoping they were out of earshot.

"Ren, I don't like where you're going with this. Helping him sounds dangerous."

"So does letting him loose and hoping he doesn't come back."

Joe nodded as she grabbed a fistful of hair, hoping to shake loose the anxiety that was building. "Fine. So what's the plan?"

"We help him however we can. But the journal doesn't leave this house." The moment she said it, she heard the chair creak behind them and she knew his hearing was better than average.

"What? No, you have to!"

She spun and put up her hands. "We can't. And you know why. Whatever is in this journal, there is no way we can just hand it over."

Tau stammered, Ren closing the gap. "If they kidnapped your sister, where do they draw the line?"

"But Panya, she can't just —"

"She won't. We'll find a way to help her."

He looked up, his eyes glittering – partly in sorrow, but partly in hope.

* * * *

Tau huffed as he dragged another large box, putting it on a growing stack on the narrowing stairwell. He wiped at the sweat prickling on his brow and moved to grab another box they had pushed toward the opening. He was mesmerized as he watched them work, moving tirelessly as they pulled down one box after the next, poring over the contents and – with unexpected regularity – forcing down the lid with a huff and a grunt of frustration. Each box was shoved away with the same animosity and rejection, making a train wreck configuration leading up to the doorway where Tau stood now. He looked on, a sense of self-consciousness clinging to him and he realized his energy was starting to wane and these girls showed no signs of slowing. In fact, they looked like they were settling into their stride. Joe pulled another box down, dropping it between them as Ren grabbed the lid and looked at the manifest. For the umpteenth time, Ren read the contents of the manifest while Joe picked through, sorting between books that might be of use and those that would be no help.

"Wizard of Oz?" Ren looked over the top of the list with curiosity as Joe moved a couple books and pulled out a large novel wrapped in plastic. She turned it over in her hands and whistled her approval. It was weathered, but the pages still looked healthy, as did the binding.

"Looks like an early edition." She set it to the side gently with the other items of disinterest. "Next."

"Three books by Winston Churchill." Her eyes widened, flicking between Joe's search and the rest of the list.

Joe held one, furrowing her brow as she shifted books from one pile to the next, finally finding a second. "I have two. The other one is probably at the bottom." She set them aside with the rest and Ren fought the urge to scream blasphemy. Joe made a sound and withdrew a wrapped parcel. "Maybe – no. Not it."

"What's that one?"

Joe looked at the letters and recognized Mariel's hand. "It says 'Voynich Manuscript, Second Edition.'"

"What?" Ren grabbed the parcel, forgetting for a moment about reverence and stared at the words. "That's impossible!"

"Not really. You'd be amazed at some of the crap Mariel has stowed away in these rooms."

"But the Voynich Manuscript is one of a kind..." Ren drifted. She was sitting on a secret that could single-handedly start her career as a historian – and she couldn't say a word about it. Joe ignored the earth-shattering revelation going on in front of her and retrieved the parcel, placing it on the pile with two Churchills and a Baum.

"Obviously not, because we have one. What's next?"

* * * *

Night passed in a blur and morning greeted them without ceremony. All three stood on uncertain legs, rocking in an imaginary wind if they stood still for too long. No one had heeded when the call for sleep came. They continued to work, moving and examining boxes until there were none remaining. All the shelves were bare, the walkway crammed with boxes that would eventually need to find their way back inside. For now, they waited, looking out over the common room.

The only time sleep came was when it forced itself upon them. All at once, Ren had been in the middle of lugging out another box when the sensation over took her. She leaned onto the shelf, her knees bracing on a shelf beneath and suddenly she was drifting away. It was warm, soft, and incredibly comfortable – the kind of sleep that could only be better enjoyed if she were awake for it. Wonderful though it was, it was fleeting. She shifted too far to the right and her knees buckled. The sensation of falling was all she needed to bring her back to full alert for a while.

Each of them had moments like that, more than once through the night. By the end of the search, they were limping along. The well-oiled machine of the overnight was a hobbled jalopy today. They had persisted, forcing themselves onward to finish the task. Coming up empty was not something they expected, nor was it something they were ready to handle as frayed and worn down by exhaustion as they were. They had moved to the common room to sit and consider their next move – and passed out again, this time comfortably.

Ren woke to a shuddering in the house. It clattered and vibrated in its place. She heard it ring out three times before her brain finally pulled itself from its sleepy fog. Her eyes opened. Tau was standing in front of Mariel's office, one tight fist around the knob as he put a firm shoulder to the door, trying to hold to it to soften the impact.

He's trying not to wake us. I can't tell if that's sweet or shady.

She sat up, watching him teeter back before leaning into the door again.

"Ah. Hem." On any other day, she might have laughed as he jumped, losing the tough exterior and looking like a child caught in the act. "Go ahead: tell me it's not what it looks like."

He didn't reply, but he did let go of the door and step away from it. Ren stood up and wobbled for a second, then took a couple long strides in his direction.

"Did we make a mistake trusting you? Because I can certainly show you the door now."

He froze, his eyes meeting hers.

"No, please."

"Didn't we show you that we were invested yesterday? Was it not clear that we want to help? Because what I see here," Her eyes flared and he faltered, taking half a step back. "This is either blatant disrespect or outright betrayal."

"It's not either." His shoulders sank; he didn't bother to meet her eye. "I couldn't just wait for you to wake up."

"Yes, you could."

"Look Ren, I appreciate the help, but every minute wasted I risk my sister –"

He flinched as her arm snapped out to her side. She didn't move otherwise, didn't lunge to attack him. She only pointed. But her muscles vibrated with the weight of the world upon them. He looked at where she was pointing: the small ball curled up in the corner of the couch that would at some point unfurl into a full-size Joe.

"*I* am risking *mine* every minute I help you." Her arm snapped back, pointing at him. "If any of this comes back on her…" She couldn't finish the statement. Her brain reminded her how exhausted she was, her nerves were healing but still frayed. Bad thoughts could become runaway terrors in the wrong frame of mind, which she was certainly in. "Maybe you should leave."

He looked shocked, as if he might have been prepared for anything to be hurled at him right now except that. He was suddenly alert and apologetic. He turned, following as Ren moved past him, through the kitchen.

"No, wait. Please!" He tried to stop himself as she turned around.

"We'll keep looking, but you can't stay."

"But if they come looking for me…"

"Then maybe you can ask them where they saw it last. We're not hiding it from you, obviously. And we are running out of places to look."

"But —"

"No." She guided him to the side entrance, opening the door. "Get us a lead. Anything would help."

He nodded, begrudgingly moving toward the door. He paused on the stoop as he passed through the threshold.

"Come back tomorrow. And cross your fingers that we come across something in your absence."

He half smiled over his shoulder. "I will."

Ren closed the door, twisting the lock. She stepped back into the kitchen, grabbing a bag of sliced deli pepperoni from the fridge as she stared out the window, watching him move across the lawn. She followed his movements from window to window, watching as he shuffled slowly. He didn't pause or look back, but he certainly took his time making his way off the property. It was that moment, as he was about to vanish out of sight, that Ren got an idea. It was as stupid as it was brilliant, but she needed to act fast.

She tossed the bag of lunchmeat onto the coffee table and lunged onto the couch. The ball in the corner barely stirred, even when Ren grabbed it with both hands.

"Joe, listen, I need to hurry." There was a grunt and a growl in reply. She growled in response and grabbed a marker from the table. In a hurried scrawl, she left a message on Joe's arm, certain the girl would find it when she woke – she almost had to.

Chasing Tau. Back soon.

I hope. She wanted to add, but knew the panic it would cause. All the same, she swallowed hard and looked at the windows again. She grabbed a jacket as she sprinted through the rooms, slipping out the door and trying to catch his trail before it went cold.

* * * *

Ren darted carefully across the neighborhood lawns as she moved down the block. She had lost sight of Tau, and had no idea if she was catching up to him or not. She darted through bushes and behind trees, trying to stay behind cover as she attempted to catch up. The morning light was growing, but the sun had not yet climbed over the horizon. She lost track of how far she'd traveled, but suddenly the foliage simply vanished. Just as the neighborhood gave way to the shopping district to the south, to the north it ended in the blight of industry.

Abandoned garages, enormous industrial machines and barren, broken concrete sprawled before her, contained safely behind rusty barbed fences. She looked in all directions but could see no trail to follow and no leads. She had lost him, but she was certain he headed in this direction.

The area seemed a far cry from civilization. It would be a good hiding place for someone resourceful – a thief, or perhaps a den of them.

She continued on, following the broken sidewalk and feeling like she stepped out of reality and into some dystopian fantasy. All she was missing now was some sort of nihilistic army to hunt her and the picture would be complete.

Shut up, brain. The last thing we want is a robot army hunting us.

Maybe it was paranoia, but she felt like she was already being hunted. From the moment she had stepped out into the open, the eyes had been on her. Of course, she hadn't seen them, which is why she was discounting it as paranoia. She reminded herself that paranoia did not necessarily mean she was wrong.

Rocks tumbled beyond the fence, making her jump. She snapped her head around, but saw nothing. She didn't even see the rocks; still she stared wide-eyed, hoping to catch a glimpse of… someone? Something? She strafed down the fence line, looking inward. There was, as far as she could tell, no life in the industrial park. But there were plenty of hiding places. There were more than enough hills to duck behind, plenty of machines to conceal within. And there appeared to be a large warehouse beyond the piles of stone and silt. It was mostly obscured, and Ren decided it was best not to linger on it; there would definitely be another opportunity to look into it.

She looked around again, slowly turning and heading back to civilization. Every now and again, she would be tempted, but decided it was better not to look over her shoulder. If anything were going to get the drop on her, she would rather not know.

When she was obscured by the neighborhood again, Tau stepped out of his hiding place. It hadn't been much of one, but he hadn't had much time. Ren was light on her feet – and fast. He had underestimated her once already, and it had gotten him caught. Then, she had almost gotten the drop on him here – completely inexcusable. He had ducked behind an abandoned garage across from the quarry and held his breath. Fortunately, it appeared that Ren had overestimated his skills – she was heavily focused on the quarry itself, even with its tall fence. She had almost started looking elsewhere when he threw the rock over her head into the debris. It hadn't been much of a clatter, but it was enough to pull her focus. He wasn't sure what to do beyond that – he knew he couldn't sneak up on her out in the open. There were only so many times he could distract her before she caught wise. He crouched low and waited, watching. He had expected her to search more, maybe try to find a way into the quarry – that would have been very bad. But just when he expected things to get worse for him, she turned and left.

For a moment, he just waited, certain she was going to turn back and look over her shoulder. He continued watching until she was out of sight. Even then it wasn't safe, but he had a powerful head start. He kept an eye on the tree line as he moved across the street and along the fence. He found the break in the fence line and slipped through it, scrambling into the obscurity of the quarry, making his way to the warehouse where he could check in and decide on the next course of action.

TEN

Joe saw the message some time after waking. If she had been worried when she woke up and found that neither Ren nor Tau were around, she could only call this current sensation panic. Her nerves frayed as she worried a path into the carpets and hardwoods, wandering the halls of the manor house in anything but a patient fashion.

It seemed like such a simple task: just wait around until Ren got back. The problem in Joe's brain was that she had no idea when Ren would be returning, what condition she'd be returning in, or what kind of chaos would befall the house before she returned. It had not been a great week for the Delaneys so far. Joe wasn't even sure what Mariel and Colette were up to, but she was certain that it couldn't be good news that dragged them away so abruptly, so that was one more worry on the brain. Embracing the panic of waking up alone in the middle of a crisis, she had tried both Colette and then Mariel's cell phones – to no avail. She tried to shake it off. Clearly they were still sleeping. A voice mail would only panic them. She could try again later.

In her worry and wonder, Joe had ensured that all doors and windows were locked and found her way back into the common room, staring at the wall of shelves and all of the books it housed. She often found herself here when she was aimless. She thought it was partly because it was the common room – the central hub of life in the house, but the other part was that, whether she enjoyed reading as much as her sisters, she enjoyed the cross section of history that these shelves held. Old books and new, it was a collection that was ever circulating.

Dusty but immaculate, some books were famous in recent years, others famous for all time, some completely obscure but beautifully crafted. Each a piece of art and history in its own right and as well maintained as the day it was bound. She walked up and down the wall of shelves, dragging gentle fingers along the spines, listening to the sound of her soft pads on leather and cloth spines, feeling the molded spines, the deep insets of names and titles. She closed her eyes as she often did and wandered back along another shelf, making a soft pitter-patter rhythm of fingertips hopping from book to book. And then – cold. She stopped, stepping back and looking with eyes that focused slowly as she turned to the books. She looked again, uncertain what she had touched. It had been hard, ugly. It was not the luxurious sensation of any book she knew in the Delaney library. It was an imposter and she could feel its presence creeping in, molesting her sense of calm. She couldn't see anything out of place, so she hesitantly reached along the shelf, passing fingers over the spines again. She felt along, touching with trepidation. As if the imposter could hurt her physically as well as mentally. Her fingers brushed the hard surface and she retracted quickly. She stared at it, poking it again. Tactile sensation betrayed what she saw with her own eyes. She shifted from side to side, judging it on contrasting angles. It looked just like any one of its compatriots on the shelf, exactly like them.

But one of these things is not like the other.

She sneered at the imposter and grabbed at its spine. She tried to pull it from the shelf but it would not budge. She tapped her knuckles on it and heard the solid thud as she connected. Gently, carefully, she removed its neighbors, finding that they relocated without issue.

This one definitely does not belong.

She cleared the shelf and thunked it again. It held firm to its place on the shelf. She tried to shift it, push it, and pull it, all with the same result. It seemed, somehow, to be connected directly to the shelf it rested on. She placed fingers on each of its false and uncomfortable covers, pressing and lifting directly. It gave slightly before catching, but there was definitely a space beneath it now. She screwed up her face in concentration as she wiggled the phony hardcover again. Her concentration gave way to clenched teeth, wiggling and pushing, feeling the tension appear in her muscles. All at once, the charlatan popped loose, knocking against the shelf above and getting loose from Joe's grip, clattering loudly on the empty shelf. She pulled her hand away with surprise, not sure what she expected to happen as it fell, but not wanting her precious digits anywhere near in the event of catastrophe.

Could this be what they had been looking for? Or did this house have more than one creepy secret within its walls?

Delicately, as if cradling Pandora's box, Joe carried it to the couch, setting it on the table before her as she sat and looked at it. To the casual observer, it was a book. It was old and more than a little worn. The gilt lettering was almost nonexistent on the spine, but the imprint was still there. She traced her fingers along the letters, her lips speaking the words silently.

Finnegan's Wake. Joe's nose wrinkled and she shook her head. No wonder it had gone unnoticed. She had tried reading Joyce's final novel once of her own accord. She had understood none of it, never getting beyond the first page. She'd given it up and promised never to make the mistake a second time. Now, she turned the false copy over in her hands. On the inside, where the covers should open to pages, it was flat and featureless, save for the insets where the book locked itself to the shelf. She looked it over again, looking for a way inside. The puzzle box had to open to some sort of secret, but did she dare? Was this something she was willing to handle herself? Alone?

She pushed forward, exploring the edges, feeling for some sort of clue – all the damn detective stories had clues that gave everything away, why didn't this? Did it flip? Did it slide? Maybe it lifted off? She had no idea, and the more she thought about it, the more her curiosity ate at her and she no longer needed anyone to be here when she opened it. Rather, she wanted to have the answers ready when Ren returned. She could see the seam that held the lid, or what she thought was the lid. There was no indication of a way to slip or pull it loose. Again, over and over, she rotated the forgery in her hands. It made no sense to make a container that could not be reopened. But that was exactly what made it the prize they were looking for, wasn't it?

She set it on its end, staring at the words on the spine, waiting for them to speak to her. Joe had hoped something might click in her brain, but it was a long shot – she knew little to nothing of the story, except her loathing for it. She picked it up again, holding it up at an angle to the light. There was something faded – a snake of sorts – worn away with the words and almost completely lost to obscurity. It's tail wound at the top, and the beast slithered its way down the spine into and out of the words, leading down, where it faded at the bottom edge. She considered it again. The head pointed toward the bottom corner. She positioned her fingers where the snake was staring. She pressed hard, and then twisted it in her hands, digging her nails in and pulling. She was certain the snake had to be an indicator – a clue – not just a pretty accent. Nothing gave, nothing moved. She considered one of the many heavy objects in the house she could shatter this forsaken relic with. If she wanted to destroy it, she could, but she had no desire. Like the rest of the objects in her home, she wanted to preserve this one too; to return it to its place on the shelf, minus its secrets. To do that, she needed to outsmart the puzzle box.

She looked at the back cover, where the

snake was pointing, and wanted to strangle the rotten little reptile as it taunted her. She poked and prodded, her brain boiling with frustration. Finally, she could do nothing but growl, twisting it in her hands as she pushed and pulled in various directions. There was a small but obvious knock that rang out, and she stopped. The front cover had slid away from the spine. It was barely a centimeter, but as seamless as the rest of it appeared to be, this was definitely something new. And it was certainly enough to rekindle the fire in Joe's heart. She turned it, pressing again. The back cover followed suit, slipping away from the spine. She was getting somewhere now. She braced it between her knees, holding it tight as she pressed her palm against the spine, hoping she was pushing from the right direction, hoping this was the next step. She almost dropped the book when it creaked out loud. The sound was awful, but the spine had definitely budged. She pushed again, cringing at the sound. It was rough wood rubbing against itself. She clenched her teeth against it and continued sliding the spine up. She removed the spine and set it on the table.

She looked down at the opening that had

appeared before her, spying into the interior compartment. She brushed her fingers over the object inside. It was a silk cloth wrapping that held its contents fast in the space. There were spaces on the top and bottom that she could almost slip a fingernail into. Slowly and with great determination, she managed to pick a corner of the silk handkerchief, pulling gently, grabbing a little more with each insistent tug.

Though it seemed like all progress had come to a standstill, eventually she worked the edge loose enough to hold solidly between her fingers, tugging until it tugged back. The silk was taut and Joe worried she would tear it. She had no idea if the clue was the fabric itself or the object within. She could risk neither. She turned the box over and started from the beginning on the other end, teasing the fabric out of its hiding place. Obsession had sunk its claws deep into Joe. She had already managed great success; she would not give in when she was so close. Her face tightened as she worked, the world around her fading away into obscurity. Here there was only the box, its contents and Joe. Nothing else mattered. She picked at the fabric, tugging until she could use it to pry the entire parcel loose. She pulled the object out, a large flat rectangle wrapped in silk, just smaller than the novel it pretended to be. Joe was almost positive she knew what she was holding without seeing it.

"What are you doing?"

Joe screamed, the box and the parcel clattering to the floor. She shook with tension and the aftershock of fear, quickly rebounding with a frustrated response as she stared up at Ren, whose surprise might have rivaled her sister's.

"Who just sneaks up like that? Why didn't you say you were back?"

"I did. You didn't answer." Ren peeked around Joe, looking at what she had dropped. "What's that?"

"It might be our mystery," she retrieved her prize from the floor and caressed the silk wrappings that kept it safe. She bent again and picked up the false book in her other hand. "It was hiding inside a puzzle."

"Really," Ren took the container from her, turning it over in her hands before looking back to Joe. "Really?"

Joe nodded.

"Aren't mysteries usually wrapped in enigmas?"

Joe snatched the container back, slipping the spine back into place. "I guess whoever built this didn't know that's how it's done." She snapped the covers back into their rightful places and passed the completed puzzle box back to Ren. She ran her hands over it, feeling how tightly sealed the object was. Even watching how it went back together, she wasn't sure she could repeat the process to open it. She was doubly sure she wouldn't have figured it out on her own without a tantrum – or three. "It's elaborate, isn't it?"

"That's putting it lightly. How did you find it?"

"It was an accident. I was just trying not to worry about you." She pointed at the shelf it had come from. "I guess it's true what they say about 'the minute you stop looking'."

"Remind me to try that the next time I need to make progress on anything." She leaned against Joe and gave her a smile. "Can we unwrap our present now?" She eyed the parcel with an eagerness usually reserved for children who sneak glimpses of their presents before Christmas.

"Yes, but we have to gentle," Joe tugged the package away from her sister's greedy hands; wanting to make sure her instructions were understood. "Gen. Tly. Please."

Ren surrendered, realizing that her enthusiasm might not be appreciated with as much effort as Joe had put into figuring this puzzle out on her own. She leaned back, watching as Joe unfolded the fabric, one silken fold at a time.

Fold by fold, Joe opened the scarf to see a small leather-bound book within. It was so immaculately preserved. It had a natural curl to the covers, probably from years of use and handling, but the pressure of being contained for so many years had held it to almost-original flatness. As Joe lifted the book in her hands, preparing to open the cover, Ren instinctively closed in, almost perched on Joe's shoulder to get a good view. Joe cracked open the journal, holding it delicately so she wouldn't damage any of the pages as she flipped through. On the inside cover was the same cursive scrawl that was displayed all over the house. In his own hand, he had written:

The Personal and Private Reflections of Gen. William Delaney, 1856 —

Ren's heart stopped dead in its tracks. The snipe hunt was over. Joe looked over her shoulder and tapped that blank spot that was usually reserved for an end date. They both knew the answer that filled in the blank. They knew when he had died, and how. It was obvious that his dying thoughts were not to update his journal. But the question now was who had hidden it and why? What were they going to find in this journal that would make it so valuable?

Joe flipped the pages slowly, gently, using the silk to keep her fingers from tarnishing the aged pages. To Ren, it sounded brittle like rice paper; thin antique pages that reminded her of her grandmother's bible. She flicked a smile as she read over Joe's shoulder, the sounds and smells of her grandmother's living room coming back to her, thoughts she hadn't actually had for years. Not since she was a child. Exploring old familiars did that to her, always possessing her and pulling her through the current of time to another place. Joe had stopped on a page for too long and Ren felt the need to nudge her from behind, a less than subtle hint that Joe quickly picked up on with a labored sigh.

"You can't rush perfection, you know."

"I don't want perfection, I want answers. The truth is never pretty anyway, so it can't be perfect."

Josephine nodded. Though brash, Ren wasn't far off track. They needed answers. The whole story, unfortunately, would have to wait. Answers always had a way of creating more questions than they bothered to solve. She flipped the pages, scanning for key words. Anything that might give them a clue as to what made this journal special enough to be buried away. From what she could gather, it really was his own personal thoughts; things that he could not allow to see the light of day.

Private thoughts, dark thoughts.

Here, he tucked away his doubts about the military and political movements of the nation. He had seen something coming to a head. If only he had known that terrible disagreement that was going to wind up being the Civil War, but he hardly had to worry about that. The fever had taken him before he had to see his doubts realized and his fears materialized. She flipped ahead, as rapidly as the brittle pages would allow. Her brain delayed, sending the impulse a moment too late. Her eyes had seen something but it hadn't fully registered. She carefully backtracked.

"What? Did I miss something?" Ren leaned in more, gripping Joe's shoulders as she turned the pages in reverse.

"I saw something."

"What?" Ren tried leaning in as far as she could physically do so. Joe shook her shoulders, trying to shift Ren's weight a bit.

"Patience…" She couldn't concentrate on both Ren's vulturing and concentrate on the scripted pages at the same time. She scanned flipping back through slowly, reading the lines in reverse. Right to left and bottom to top, taking one word at a time, making sure she didn't miss it again. When she finally found it, she stared, believing her eyes even less now than when she first suspected. She wanted to get away from the book as quickly as possible; it had to be causing hallucinations.

"This can't be right." Joe pointed at the

words and held the page up to Ren. "Read it. Tell me I'm not crazy."

"You know I have trouble with his –" Ren eyes were slits of concentration, widening with the same disbelief Joe's held. "Does that say Eunice Abernathy?"

Joe nodded. "Maybe it's coincidence? Or a family name?" She set her jaw, knowing that it was all wishful thinking. One answer, but now they had so many more questions.

Ren just stared at the name on the page and shook her head. "How is that even possible?"

"I don't know, but I'm afraid we might have to ask her."

ELEVEN

Ren was up bright and early. Normally, such things were almost impossible to fathom. It wasn't that she preferred night to day, she rather enjoyed the sunshine but she had noted time and again that it took that much more coffee to function earlier on. But today was going to be something spccial. She skipped down to the kitchen, starting an extra strong pot of coffee, and took her time getting ready for the day.

After an extra hot shower, she slipped into a nice pair of breezy slacks and a light grey blouse. She threw her black velvet blazer on over the ensemble and finished the outfit with a silver chain. She smiled as she regarded herself in the mirror, swaying back and forth, amused by the way the jacket tails would billow slightly when she turned. Fun, yet completely professional. She moved toward the door and paused with her fingers on the knob.

Are you sure you're ready to do this? What are you going to do if this really is as big as you imagine?

Her thoughts nagged at her, worry and fear holding the door fast. She took a deep breath and closed her eyes. She reminded herself how far she had come in this short time. Not just anyone was able to come back for a second chance at life, much less be able to handle the news without going insane. She and Joe had managed plenty in the last handful of days on their own. Tau hadn't shown his face for two long days and not only were they able to get a better look at William's journal, but they handled a weekend with the museum open for business all on their own. If they could manage tours and questions on a staff of two, they could certainly save the world from whatever hulking evil was looming on the horizon.

She laughed to herself and twisted the doorknob, officially beginning the day.

She sat over a cup of coffee and a bagel,

reading William's secret journal with a notebook of her own right beside it. At the edge of the table, she had a couple of his journals from the museum. In her own notes, she cited pages and passages from William's various journals, trying to recreate a timeline across the collection. The "secret" journal appeared to be a place to put notes he wanted to keep off public record. She had gone between the books for half a day before she realized that he had marked every entry. Ren had enough trouble deciphering his handwriting that she hadn't noticed at first, but when he intended to switch journals mid-story, there was a small blot of ink at the end of the line. It was a small touch, practically undetectable, but one that proved to be a solid indicator. After that, it didn't take much time before she switch between books with the ease of turning a page.

In the years before the war, William had been put in charge of a company that guarded a supply line leading west. He would occasionally travel the route, guiding the caravan to the end of his jurisdiction on the trail. William found the further he travelled out into the vacant unknown; the more he found peace in his days. He had no taste for the aristocracy in the big cities. He wanted a quiet life, and thought he was close to finding it.

He took to trading with and befriending those he found on the trail, packing extra supplies to exchange for information about the area, or rare items that he could find nowhere else that he knew of. In particular, he did a lot of trading with Jacob, who seemed to know the lay of the land. Jacob had two sons and a daughter who helped him care for his stake. He spoke often of leaving the farm behind and following the stories of glory in the west. There was plenty of talk of fortune and freedom beyond the territories. William had no interest in anything that reminded him of the life he had all but abandoned in the eastern states. He was comfortable right here in the middle, somewhere he could stake a claim, settle in, and let the world grow up around him.

It was on one of his many visits that William noticed a blade hung on the wall in Jacob's home. It was a long blade, almost a foot and a half long. William had drawn a picture of it in the journal, commenting how much it reminded him of an officer's dagger upon first glance. The blade was thin with a deep black handle and "shimmered like it had a light that shone from within". William was instantly taken with it. He tried to discuss the weapon with Jacob, asking if it had been a family heirloom. Jacob refused to discuss the weapon and all polite conversation after.

A number of times, William returned to trade with Jacob, and each time their business ended when the conversation turned to the knife. But William would not let it go. There was something about it that called to him.

During a particularly bad winter, William found Jacob down on his luck. He had sent his children on earlier to trade with a fort in the north and seek refuge during the colder months. He had hoped that the soldiers would pity the children, but expected Jacob himself would have no such luck, so he remained behind. William gifted Jacob with what he needed to get through the remaining months. Jacob tried to refuse, having no way to repay him. When William insisted and began unloading, Jacob saw no other recourse, and gifted the dagger to him.

William wrote that, though grateful for the supplies, Jacob seemed insistent yet reluctant to part with the dagger. He added that Jacob's entire mood darkened as they parted ways. It worried him and he set to scheduling a return trip as soon as the he was able.

By the time he returned, luck had indeed turned on Jacob. The season had broken and spring was fighting for control over the territory. Jacob's home was a guttered ruin. The charred remains of his home and three bodies were the first things William came across on his next patrol. By whatever luck, his daughter had been spared. She was crazed, starving, and almost feral, having survived on her wits alone until the patrol discovered her in the brush. They tried to capture her, to see to her safety, but she fought them like a wild beast – until she set eyes on William. He made note that her eyes lit on the dagger and she instantly cooled. He presumed it was because she had remembered it from its time in her home. William did the only thing he could think to do: he took the young girl in. He helped bring her back to sound mind and body and, with no living relatives that she was aware of, took her in his care.

Ren continued to read, William's journal

going on to discuss his reluctant return to proper society to give his new charge a proper education and later their courtship. Ren looked over the pages again, noting that Eunice's age is never specifically discussed. With a shudder, she hoped this wasn't going to be a big ugly spot on William's permanent record. Otherwise, she spent the morning's research stunned that present-day Eunice had apparently not been lying about Grandmother Abernathy's relationship to William Delaney.

Joe dragged herself into the kitchen, not nearly as bright and alert as Ren had been all morning. She managed a pair of toaster waffles without electrocuting herself, and settled in with a cup of coffee while her breakfast warmed. She looked across the table, smirking.

"You're like a mini-Mariel."

Ren tried to stare Joe down with one of the gazes that Mariel was notorious for, but couldn't keep a straight face.

"At least we won't have to replace her."

"Oh no, she'll be there to instruct us every step of the way."

Ren hesitated. "If it gets to be too much,

we'll just mutiny."

"That sounds like a plan," Joe raised her cup in salute, then responded to the chime of the toaster. "So what adventure is William up to today?"

Ren sighed. "I really wish I hadn't read any of this myself. I mean, William is honest, but he's not painting himself in the best light. And something is definitely up."

Joe raised an eyebrow as she leaned in, waiting for the juicy bits.

"So, William meets Jacob Abernathy. Jacob had a knife William wants. Jacob is weird about it and refuses. One day, he finally forks it over. Later on, boom: everyone dies."

"Let me guess: Eunice is somehow okay?"

"Well, not okay. She's crazy and kind of beastly when he finds her. But she calms down – William says probably because of the dagger, like maybe she remembers it. Then William does the good guy thing and takes her in and introduces her to proper society and being a lady and they start a relationship."

A noise creeps up from the back of Joe's throat. "Please tell me she's legal when this happens."

Ren pauses, considering her response. "We're going to gloss over that, because then he meets Mariel."

"And we know that story: It's love at first sight, they head off again into the wilderness and find a nice place to build a house – this house – and they live happily ever after."

"Until tragedy strikes."

"I like my ending better." Joe eyes roll wide, wishing they really could ignore this part of history.

"But your ending is a romance. This is a mystery."

Joe stared at her. She knew she was supposed to ask a question, but for the life of her, she had no idea which one to start with.

Ren stabbed at the page repeatedly. "Tau is looking for a journal, but he should be looking for a knife."

Joe looked at the book again; it was slowly coming together. Very slowly. It still sounded a little like insanity to her, but Ren marched forward.

"Eunice lives with Jacob; Jacob has the

dagger. Jacob gives the dagger to William: dead Jacob. William has the dagger; and now Eunice lives with William."

It clicked and Joe slapped the table. "William takes the dagger when he goes off with Mariel!" The pieces continued to fit across her mind, the excitement draining from her face in dawning realization. "She killed them? All over a dagger?"

Ren nodded soberly. "I think so."

"We can't prove any of this."

"Yet."

"Yet?"

Ren leaned in, as if someone might be eavesdropping. "Someone is looking for this dagger. That must mean that Eunice never got it. Mariel must have it somewhere."

Joe looked like her brain was going to implode on her.

"I don't like us being in charge anymore."

* * * *

Ren spent the afternoon in the museum, dealing with visitors and counting down the hours until Abernathy's group came in. She thought it would be hard to pass the afternoon, but what time wasn't spent attending to guests was spent looking for clues that led back to the knife in question. It was dizzying, bouncing from one unanswered question to the next. She was starting to feel like she might go insane before the answers came to her. At least after today, she would be more certain of the direction they were headed in. Even if Mrs. Abernathy didn't know the whole story, Ren had every intention of asking about dear old Gran-gran. She had a hard time imagining the old woman turning down an opportunity to tell her story. She was counting on it.

What Ren didn't count on was the Daughters of the Revolution meeting without the presence of their founding member. Ren felt her face flush with disappointment and anger. But she was certain now. Abernathy creeps on them, and Tau shows up. Tau vanishes and so does she. Coincidence be damned, there was something suspect about this. She kept her calm as long as she was humanly able. The moment the last Daughter was out the door, Ren twisted the lock and flicked the lights off, moving by memory as she made a beeline for the common room.

Within, Joe had taken point on William's journals. She also had a number of other books spread out on the table with her. When she saw Ren, she leaned over the table, reorganizing everything into a sloppy cascade of books, binders and – oddly enough – picture frames.

"Before you start: no, I don't know where it is." She smiled. "Not for certain. I have my suspicions though. And," She picked up a picture of William and Mariel, arm in arm. William was in full regalia and Mariel wore a dress that Ren might be murdered for mentioning out loud. It was the parasol that made her giggle. Joe tapped the frame. On his belt, just ahead of his sword, was a dagger. It was sheathed to match the rest of the uniform, but the handle matched William's drawing. "We definitely know what we are looking for."

"There is an awful lot of time between this picture and now."

"Yes, but," She held up another framed picture, this one far more recent. Mariel looked much more like herself, standing with a group of people as they all held up a banner. Marysville

Time Capsule: 2010. Ren looked at the picture then back to the previous, trying to connect the two. Before she could admit defeat, Joe pointed again. There, partially obscured by her blazer, William's sheath hung from her belt. It looked limp, a good indicator that no dagger was sheathed in it. "That's the most recent time reference I can find. It might be the last time it was seen."

"Do you think anyone else noticed this?"

Joe shrugged. "If they had, I'm sure they've opened the time capsule by now."

"If they haven't, we need to get there first."

"Agreed."

* * * *

That night, Ren tried to sleep deep and full, but her dreams had other plans.

She stood on a worn trail in the middle of nowhere. The sun shone bright on her face, she could smell grass and flowers on the warm wind. She could also smell misery and death. She turned to see the guttered remains of a log house, the wood slat roof all but missing, the flames leaving only the edges behind. The thick wood walls still stood, but the heat emanating from the structure told Ren that it was still burning strong, regardless of what appeared to remain.

"No!"

Ren turned to see young Eunice Abernathy. Her hands and face were covered in soot, hiding most of the young girl behind a drab featureless dress and the ashen remains of her childhood home. Her eyes, however, were bright and alive. They sparkled as she protested – not at the smoldering remains of her family home, but at William. He stood, his back to Eunice, his hand outstretched to another woman.

"Mariel," Ren whispered, though no one seemed to acknowledge her. It was definitely Mariel; she looked exactly the same, like no time had passed at all. The telltale difference was her innocence. This Mariel had the glow of possibility in her eyes, no trace of the long years ahead – or behind – her. There was no mystique to this woman; she was exactly what she appeared to be.

Eunice reached out, clutching William's free arm, attempting to pull him back to her. As he fell back, Mariel held fast to his other hand. A tug of war ensued between them, a fight for William's heart and his affection. Ren watched, expecting him to lurch away from one or the other. She couldn't actually tell which as the display continued. Finally, his hands snapped up and he pulled away, reaching forward.

He reached for Ren, and she recoiled. This was not how it was supposed to happen. She wasn't going to end up with William. He seemed to be aware of this and did not try to pursue. Instead, he looked over his shoulder at the two women, both closing in, pleading for him to choose. He shook his head and pulled back the panel of his coat.

In one swift motion, there was nothing and suddenly it was there. He held the knife out, the handle facing Ren, as he lightly held the blade.

"Choose," He said. Just one word and Ren suddenly felt the weight and fear of everything weighing down on her. Mariel and Eunice both looked at her, eyes begging, reaching out as they tried to convey their worth in beating hearts and shining eyes.

Ren shook her head, trying to take another step away. William grabbed her wrist, slapping the hilt into her palm and stepping to her side.

"Choose, please," His voice sounded weary, strained. "Love can either burn quick and bright for me, or long and dull, but I cannot have both." He turned to her, but Ren could not bring herself to face him. "And I cannot, for the life of me, seem to make the right choice. Please, choose."

She looked on as they both pleaded with her, the two voices becoming one single sound. She knew how history decided this story should end, and she knew how her own fate was interwoven. It should have been easy but her heart tugged at her, telling her that it wasn't so simple. What if the roles had been reversed, would she feel differently? She wasn't sure she could do this any easier than William himself, so why was she stepping forward?

"Choose."

It was unbidden, involuntary. Ren was moving forward without any control of her own. She moved, the knife rolling between her fingers. She felt every movement, every muscle, but had no control over any of them. She stepped in front of Eunice, her face streaked with white lines cut into sooty cheeks by her tears. Ren could feel tears of her own, wanting to shut her eyes as she raised the knife above her head. She felt the muscles in her arm draw tight, clenching, as they pulled the weight of the blade down along its path.

She sat up in bed, gasping, panting, and trying to rid herself of a knife that was not there. She wiped her hands on the sheets, wishing she could shake the feeling, waiting for the guilt and the shame to ebb away with the memory of the dream. She lowered herself back onto her pillow staring at the ceiling as she both recalled the dream and willed it away. She tried to take solace in the late morning light, but there was no silver lining to speak of. She wanted nothing to do with these horrible thoughts.

She thought she heard the echo of her dream through her wall. William's voice and... Joe's? Ren sat up and listened again. No, it wasn't a dream. Joe was talking with someone. Ren snatched up a hoodie to throw over herself and stepped out into the hall. She let the door close harder than she had actually intended, but it stopped the conversation and let Joe know she wasn't on her own any longer.

Ren looked down over the rail of the staircase as they both looked up at her. Tau smiled and gave her a half wave as Joe tried to speak an entire volume with one exasperated stare.

"I thought the cat was supposed to come back the very next day," she stretched as she came down the stairs. His smile faded, which was the desired effect. "What did I miss out on?"

"I've been trying to explain to him that we've been making progress with the journals we have, but it's slow going." The eyes continued to scream their story. Ren got the jist well enough: *I haven't told him anything.*

"And I've been saying that if either of you were better at what you're supposed to be doing here, I'd have my sister back already," He tried to be casual, but his words still shimmered with the venom of a bitter man.

Joe spun and slapped him in the chest with one of William's heavier journals. "It's aged handwriting. Old ink and quill writing from two hundred years ago. It might as well be Sanskrit for as well as we can read it."

Ren tried to stifle a laugh. "I still wouldn't

wish Sanskrit on us."

Joe let the book go, watching Tau fumble with it. She ran a hand through her hair and stormed off to the kitchen. Ren watched him struggle with William's penmanship for a moment before giving him reprieve.

"We're trying. You could be more understanding."

His jaw tightened as his eyes snapped up to meet hers. "You're not the one running out of time."

"I know that. It might help if we had a better idea of what we're hunting for."

"I told you –"

"What *they* told you. But where has that gotten us? What's the end game? What do they need?"

"If I knew that –"

Ren snatched the book from him. "And why don't you? We've been here, turning this whole place upside down *for you* for two days. Where have you been?"

"I've been trying to get answers – or at least more time."

"Then shouldn't you keep trying that? We

could use a little more direction to go on."

"I can help you here. Three of us can cover more ground faster." Ren felt her stomach knot. She didn't know how she could have an actual conversation with Joe as long as he was around, and he didn't seem to have any interest in leaving. And she still didn't know if it was genuine concern or if he was spying on them.

She was glad Joe was smarter – or at least more determined – than she was. The false book was back together and the shelf had been returned to its original condition. She didn't know where Joe had moved the journal to, but she was determined not to look very hard for it today.

She gave him a defeated look. "I understand your concerns, but I haven't forgotten how this all started either. You broke in here. As far as I am concerned, that still makes you more the problem than the solution. We have turned this place upside down looking for god knows what. How are you even sure it's here?"

Joe returned with a serving tray: cups, sugar, cream and a steaming pot of morning joy. She cleared her throat as she stepped between them, knowing that Ren had taken her position and it was up to Joe to play the other side. From what she had heard from the kitchen, she was a little relieved: she made a better good cop than bad cop.

"If you want to make yourself useful, and you don't seem to think that we can do this job on our own, then you can start bringing boxes up from the basement. One at a time, for us to go through. *Again.*"

Where he didn't waver in the face of Ren's opposition, he visibly winced at Joe's gentle push into reasonable doubt. He looked caught between guilt and punishment, but he nodded slowly. Joe waved a hand and made him follow. She showed him to the stairs beyond the kitchen. Two steps led down to a landing where the side entrance waited. The basement was at the bottom of the landing, fourteen steps down, running below the kitchen and to the far end of the house. Perhaps at one point, the intent had been to run a subterranean level under the length of the house, but such a project had never been completed. In recent years, Mariel had finished the basement to guard it against the elements and make it more fitting for storage. Of all the work she had done, Joe noticed that she had never added any additional lighting, so the basement had a permanent creepiness to it, caused by the tall shelves and the single light source down below.

Joe knew very well what was down there; she had helped stock the basement in the first place. It had been a long and laborious task to decide what could stand to be kept in the basement, in the event of a flood, or severe moisture. No documents, no fabrics, no photos. Metal and wood items needed to be packaged properly, but were likely safe. Really, most of it was secondary storage for the boring stuff no one wanted to see, but would be rude to throw out. All in all: a wild goose chase.

"You can start wherever you like, but there's an order, so whatever you take out has to go back to the same spot."

He nodded and took the stairs with heavy footfalls. Joe tried to move back to the common room with a normal gait. She wanted nothing more than to run and fill her sister in on every word in her brain, every thought that had passed since this morning. Instead, she kept her calm.

Ren opened her mouth and Joe immediately held up a finger. First, to her mouth to hush Ren, then gently to her ear followed by a thumb pointing behind her.

Of course, Ren nodded, *his stupid hearing.*

It was going to be an impossibly annoying day.

* * * *

What might have been a ten minute conversation in real-time ended up dragging out through the length of the day. They debated the pros and cons of telling Tau about the journal, but certainly nothing beyond that. In the end, they decided that he didn't need to know anything until they were sure of where he stood with them, and they with him.

"It's possible that his sister *is* in danger, but he's not as worried as he tries to be," Joe had to lean in, speaking as quickly as she could do in a whisper. By noon, they were speaking in hushed tones as if it were a second language. It turned into a game for them, even testing his hearing, challenging him to hear them through background noise, playing the radio, anything they could think of. His hearing was impeccable, but it had its limits. In the basement, beneath solid hardwood, he was at a severe disadvantage of not only having to move around heavy boxes, but their voices did not resonate. Still, there was no reason to tempt fate with standard volume.

They took a quick break for lunch, and then got back into the thick of things. More than once they found an object in one of the crates that would be a surprising addition to the showcases, and they wondered why Mariel hadn't put it out for display. Notes and speculations were both made, and they continued with the task at hand: pretending to look for something that they'd already hid elsewhere.

By midafternoon, they had pushed Tau to his physical limit. He was staggering as he lugged the boxes, which meant that each new trip, they endangered another box of artifacts. It wasn't worth the risk to continue pushing him, even if they were actually enjoying themselves for the time being.

"Tau, let's call it a day," Joe gestured to the couch and though he played tough for a moment, he took the offer and collapsed, stretching sore muscles as he sprawled. An idea occurred to her as she watched him sink into the cushions. She reached out and cuffed Ren in the shoulder. "I'm going to run and get us some takeout."

Ren reflexed, wanting to hit her back for the sudden sharp tingling in her upper arm. At the look in Joe's eyes, she knew better than to punish her for what must be a brilliant scheme. Instead, she clapped and stood up. "Chinese, or pizza?"

They both turned to Tau, who was so weary he didn't even realize the question was being passed to him.

"No worries, I'll figure it out." Joe ran upstairs after her money and before Ren could protest, she was already making her way to the door. "I'll be back in a flash."

"Wait, what do we do till then?"

Joe stuck out her tongue.

"Play house."

TWELVE

Joe smiled, a spring in her step as she flicked through her phone and ordered a pizza from her favorite place. They did something magical with the sauce that they claimed was an "old family recipe," but she was pretty sure it was a low dose narcotic. There was no other way to explain how tomato puree could be so addicting.

The second reason to call Papa Merrin's Pizzeria was the route to get there. Between Papa Merrin's and Delaney House was the huge urban forest of Swinton Woods. Three hundred fifty twisting acres cut through the middle of Marysville, offering the beauty and serenity of nature without wandering too far from the safety of the city. Also safeguarded by Swinton Woods was the Marysville time capsule. Joe knew there wouldn't be time to just dig it up; the capsule was supposed to survive one hundred years. If they were going to open it up and peek inside, they were going to have to plan.

She could, however, peek to make sure no one else had disturbed it.

She diverted from the city sidewalks onto a cobblestone path that led through the park. She passed park benches and pedestrian rest areas. It was surprising that more people didn't take the time to at least walk through the forest. Something about the woods swallowed the city sounds, giving the illusion that she had left civilization behind. She enjoyed passing through, but too much time in the park gave her a creepy feeling. She always felt like she had overstayed her welcome and the forest was giving her the cold shoulder in the hope that she'd leave. She was never brave enough to see what happened if she actually stayed too long.

She came to the large fountain much faster than she expected to. It was a pristine wishing pool that people threw change into all summer long, before the city came and emptied the fountain for the winter. Residents called it the Founders Fountain, referring to the brass plaques in the stonework that circled the fountain, commemorating the town's founders. Joe looked around; the time capsule had been laid to its long rest somewhere in the fountain square.

Joe twirled as she wandered around the fountain, finally finding the sealed plate dug into a small hill at the edge of the stone walkway. She knelt, reaching out and measuring the bolts against her thumb. If they had to use tools, she could at least approximate, right? She leaned in further; digging her fingers around the lip, curious about how thick the lid was –

A sudden blast of cold set her on edge. She stood up and stepped backward.

No, she didn't. Not willingly, anyhow. Cold hands had shoved her away from the capsule and she stumbled. Joe's eyes darted as she tried to see something that was obviously not there.

She was conscious of every movement she made now. She took half a step toward the capsule again. She looked everywhere, her head turning in a slow figure eight.

"Um, I'm sorry?" Joe wasn't known for her

clairvoyance, and had no idea how to deal with ghosts, if that's what this was. The closest thing to a supernatural experience, after Delaney House, was Tau. She was still a long way from her ghost-busting merit badge.

"Leave us."

She stopped, listening for more. There hadn't even been a breath of warning before the voice came. It was possible that it was all in her head, psychically. She wasn't going to rule anything out yet.

"Who is 'us'? Why do I need to leave? Can you tell me?" Joe knew how ridiculous she would appear to passersby, but there were none to speak of. No one to catch her talking to herself for her five minutes of internet fame. She was, as far as she could *see*, alone.

She took another step forward and a deep wide cold spot grew on her chest. She stopped moving, either the cold or the contact made her stop breathing as well. She swallowed hard. Her mouth had gone dry. She forced herself to inhale.

"I'm not here to –"

A face appeared right in front of her, mere inches from her own. It was so white it was almost glowing. With the exception of the deep blue eyes within the white mask, it was virtually featureless. Passive and featureless, Joe believed it might be the most angelic sight she could ever imagine. And she was correct until the face bared teeth.

"We know what you are here for!" It definitely spoke, though she didn't see its mouth move. It snarled silently, a white hand appearing on her chest. It poured cold into her, burning right down to her heart. Joe stumbled back, losing her footing against the wide wall around the fountain. She yelped and spun, expecting something worse, but it was only the fountain, gurgling and spurting water into the air. She spun back and whatever it had been was gone. She didn't need to be told again to move along. She would tempt fate another day.

She rubbed her chest trying to work warmth back into it as she turned tail toward home.

The fountain was long out of sight when she realized that somewhere in the world, a delicious ham and pepperoni pizza with extra cheese was waiting for her to collect. She growled, wanting to spend no more time in the Swinton Woods, but she really wanted her pizza. She felt the cold radiating from her chest and realized that if anything could cure what ailed her, Papa Merrin's would do the trick, or there was no cure.

* * * *

Joe managed to get the pizza back to Delaney House without further incident, but as the sun set and the shadows grew longer, the more she was certain someone – or some*thing* – was following her. Every half block she would spin in a circle, continuing her momentum, just in case she turned and someone was actually there. Every time she turned, however, the streets were as clear as the last time. She didn't even bother to come in through the back door. She rang the bell at the front and waited on timid tiptoes bouncing in place until the deadbolt slid away.

Ren opened the door, sarcastic lines playing on her tongue ever since the doorbell chimed. One look at Joe's face cast the clever words away, never to be uttered aloud.

"Joe? Get in here!" She tugged the girl's shoulder, not meaning to bark orders. Joe was already half in the door by the time Ren reached for her. "Are you okay?"

"I'm fine." She shook her head and took a deep breath. Ren's eye insisted and Joe shot a glance at the doorway beyond. Her voice dropped to the softest whisper she could manage. "We're on the right track."

She moved into the common room, watching as Tau was already sitting up, the scent of pizza tingling his nostrils.

"That smells so good," He licked his lips, then gave Joe the same look Ren had used in the doorway. "Everything alright?"

Joe stopped for a second, hunched over the table opening the box. "Some creepster was following me on the way back. Gave me the heebies, that's all."

Whether Tau really was a charlatan or a good guy mixed up in something bad, it was almost impossible to determine at this point. Sometimes he seemed so carefree, or just plain careless, that there was no way he could be in the amount of trouble he claimed. But then he would pull a brotherly move like going to the window and making sure there was no one lurking that made him seem like he really might be that guy he said he was. It made Joe's head throb, more than the idea of being frozen into a statue in the middle of Swinton Woods. She wasn't sure what she had encountered, but she was convinced it had the ability to turn creatures to stone. Or ice, which made more sense with the chilling sensation that still tingled against her chest.

Ren arrived with plates and paper towels. Joe stole a large piece of the pie and sank into a chair. She was happy that it was still warm, but not to the point where the cheese burned her mouth. This was just south of the perfect temperature. She chewed and swallowed, voicing her approval as she stuffed another mouthful between her teeth. Perhaps it was the secret ingredient, or maybe it was just magic in general, but the more pizza she devoured, the less she could feel of the place the forest spirit touched her.

The rest of the meal was shared in silence. Ren and Joe could not discuss Joe's trip because of Tau, and they had nothing left to discuss with him. Tau himself was worn down from the day and almost welcomed the silence to relax against. The pizza filled the rest of his thoughts until none remained between them.

Ren stuck out her belly and slapped the sides of it. "Oh my god, that was the best pizza ever."

The other two could only groan an agreement, Joe slowly swinging her legs around from a seated position to cradle herself in the lap of her chair, ready to slip into a long, deep food coma. Ren didn't want to rush Tau out into the night so quickly after dinner, but she did want to talk to Joe. The look on her sister's face when she opened the door was still etched into her mind. It was not casual fear that was on her face. What had she seen? What did she find?

Without any sort of pressure, Tau stood up, stretching.

"Thanks for the pizza. I should take off. I'm not going to be any more use to you tonight." Ren nodded, standing up. Joe waved groggily, her head lolling back against her shoulder as she folded her arms back around her chilled body.

Ren followed Tau to the front door, dragging her feet, feeling the comforting weight of her own food coma looming.

"Thanks, for all your help today. You deserve a good night's sleep." Ren half smiled as she leaned against one of the displays. Tau opened the door.

"I'm sure I'll get it. Tomorrow?"

Ren nodded and watched him hop down the steps, letting gravity do most of the work till he got to the bottom. Then he strolled slowly down the walk. Ren had no intention, nor any desire to pursue him. She closed the door and twisted the lock, still not certain about him. She was glad the cat puns were slowing.

He's going home for a catnap.

She shook her head and turned her attention back to the Joe's mystery.

"Alright, I want to hear what happened." She called loudly as she entered the room, but Joe didn't budge. She crept over, slipping into the chair in the opposite pose, so she faced Joe. "No nap till story time is over."

She put a shoulder into Joe's hip, watching the girl bounce. Her head rolled back a little and the smile faded from Ren's mouth. Joe's lips were purple, and her skin pale – more than was the norm. Ren reached out, her fingers touched clammy skin and she drew back. She jumped up and held her sister's face.

"Joe? Joe! Don't you do this to me. Wake up!" She tapped Joe's cheeky lightly, patting out an intense rhythm.

"So tired. Let me sleep." Joe mumbled, trying to brush Ren off weakly.

"Oh no, I've seen far too much TV for that." She grabbed Joe, pulling her up to the edge of the chair and letting out a great huff as she hoisted the cooling body over her shoulders. "You are going to owe me so much for this."

Step by step, she made her way across a room far too big for this much weight. Opting for Mariel's master bedroom instead of attempting to tackle the stairs, she hoped Mariel didn't believe in locking her own door.

She let the doorframe bear part of their shared weight for a moment while she tried the door. It swung easy on oiled hinges. Ren thanked all the gods in all the pantheons. She let momentum carry them into the room and threw Joe onto the bed. Her dark hair was wet from cold sweat and her breath was shallow. Grabbing the girl's limp legs, she worked off Joe's shoes and her socks. Then she worked Joe out of her jacket, trying to focus but she couldn't help think the worst as her fingers brushed against the wet cold skin. She had to distract herself, and wanted to reach Joe at the same time, and pull her back to the surface.

"While it is true that I spent a majority of my time chasing handsome gentlemen, this does not mean that I don't appreciate the fairer sex. I mean, I certainly do, but Joe, this is probably the laziest way anyone has ever gotten me into a bedroom. Wake up!"

She didn't respond, not that Ren really expected a miracle. She worked Joe out of her tight jeans, swearing that the girl would never leave the house in anything tighter than sweats ever again. She pulled Joe up, cradling her as she worked her top over her head. She pulled the covers back on Mariel's bed, and rolled Joe into place on the pillow.

As she pulled away, Ren felt a cold chill work its way up her spine. At the cleft of Joe's breasts, resting comfortably on her pale skin was a dark bruise in the shape of a long-fingered hand. It pressed against her sternum, branching up and out across her chest. What had happened out there?

Ren tucked Joe into bed, pulling the blankets tight around her. When she was snug, Ren rushed out of the room, making her way to the kitchen. She twisted the hot water open on full in the sink. She got two large freezer bags and filled them, wrapping them in a kitchen towel and hoped that improvisation was enough. She took them back to Mariel's room.

She placed the bags on top of Joe, keeping a blanket between them for added insulation. The last thing she wanted to do was harm when she thought she was helping.

But what happens when they cool off?

She shook her head, laughing to ease the tension. She walked around to the opposite side of the bed, facing away from Joe.

"This is *seriously* the laziest play that has ever worked on anyone." She could feel her pulse quickening as she undressed. She tried to play it off as concern for Joe – which was not false, just... inaccurate.

Ren slipped under the covers and slid up against Joe, shuddering slightly as her warm skin made contact with flesh that seemed almost waxy in its cooled state. She rolled Joe, pressing closer, holding her makeshift hot compress against Joe's body. She rested her cheek against Joe's over her shoulder and whispered gently, trying to ease the tension for herself and hopefully lessen the shock when Joe came to.

"Just remember that it's not what it looks like – ok, it's *exactly* what it looks like, but not that way. I'm trying to help. I don't know what else to do, Joe. I took some first aid classes when I was younger, when I was a babysitter. They just told us what to do, then gave us a multiple-choice test. That's it! That's everything I am basing this attempt at life saving on. Well, that and television. It can't all be wrong, can it?"

There was no response, just soft shallow breath, barely perceptible in the arms that held Joe close.

"You can't leave me, Joe. You were the first thing I found in this world. You rescued me, now I get to rescue you. That's how this plays out, you hear?" Her chin quivered, and she felt flush, but she hoped that the heat coming to the surface would help. At least that thought made it okay to be on the verge of tears right now. "You don't get to leave. I –" Ren swallowed, feeling the tears run as she blinked, holding Joe tighter. "I need you to stay right here."

THIRTEEN

At some point between the emotional overload and the general exhaustion of the day, Ren fell asleep. When she woke, it was slowly, her faculties trying to fill in the missing information. At some point, she had moved to lying on her back, and Joe had turned and was pressed into Ren's side. One hand she could feel was threaded with one of Joe's while the other felt like it was just gone. After a moment of inward panic, she realized that it must be under Joe and had gone numb. She moved her fingers reflexively, trying to get the blood and feeling back in them. It was a bizarre sensation knowing she was touching something, but completely unable to identify what it was. Joe emitted a sleepy noise and Ren turned to meet her face to face.

Joe smiled sleepily. "I'm not sure what to ask first: Why are we in bed mostly naked, or why you are squeezing my butt."

Ren retracted her hands, wide-awake and flush with embarrassment. Then, the reason they were here crept back to her and she wrapped her arms around Joe, squeezing her tight and kissing her hard on the cheek.

"You're okay? I didn't think you were going to make it." She held Joe, pulling her, pushing her, prodding, playing the frantic mother making sure her child is still in one piece after a playground fall. "I was so scared."

"Ren, it's okay. I'm fine." Joe took the frantic shaking hands in hers and held them close. "I don't actually remember much of last night. I vaguely remember getting back here after…" Her voice drifted off, and her mind when to a faraway place. Her eyes grew wide with the dark memories and she squeezed Ren's hands tighter against her. Ren held tight to her, trying to be her anchor.

"Joe?"

"I remember…" Her eyes snapped back to

reality and the safety of the present moment. "Something is in the park, protecting the time capsule."

"Something." Ren repeated, almost hypnotically as she reached out and moved the blankets. The handprint was still on Joe's chest, though she seemed completely unaware of it. Ren touched it, and Joe looked down, trying to see. "Something very dangerous. Do you think the knife is there?"

Joe nodded. "If it's not, something else ridiculously significant is being hidden there." She looked down again, only able to see part of the mark, a dark blot on her chest. "Is it bad?"

Ren smiled. "Not as bad as things got last night."

Joe reached out and touched her cheek, holding her gaze for a long minute. "Thank you." She looked like she was going to say more, but spied something over Ren's shoulder. She cocked her head and her eyebrows lowered as she considered. She rolled back looking around the room, her head snapping back to Ren.

"Mariel's room?"

"It was either this or chancing breaking our

necks on the stairs."

She paused to weigh the options, her reaction scaling down from 'Oh god, my parents are home!' to 'You probably made the right call.'

"We still shouldn't hang out here too long." She shoved at the covers then pulled them back in place, remembering just how bare she was. "Cover your eyes."

Ren laughed. "What?"

"Cover your eyes."

"Joe, really. I saw pretty much everything last night."

"I was unconscious!"

"It's nothing to be ashamed of. Pretend you're in a bikini."

"How about you close your eyes and pretend they're open."

Ren got in one last eye roll before she shut her eyes and put a hand over them. "Alright, the coast is clear." She had barely begun her sentence before the bed began to shake. Joe scrambled and the door flew open. She sprinted through the house with an armload of damp clothes, chased all the way up the stairs and to her room by Ren's hysterical laughter.

* * * *

After a proper morning routine, and enough time doing who-knows-what behind closed doors, Joe appeared finally ready to see Ren face to face without a deep crimson blush. Though Ren did make a note that if she stared too long, Joe had to look away and her face would flush all over again. She tried to keep it to a minimum, but it was almost too much fun to avoid doing.

Through the morning, they debated back and forth what Joe had been confronted with in Swinton Woods. The only thing they were sure of was that they had no idea what it was, or where to start looking for answers. The hope was that it was something they could understand and, well, that was about as far as the plan went. Even if they figured out what it was, could it be reasoned with? Could it be beaten? *Should* it be beaten? If it was defending the time capsule, they could be certain the knife was in safe hands.

This line of questions spiraled out of control, and they realized they were probably worse off than when this had all started. But would they even have the courage to ask Mariel about all of this if she were here? They'd have to answer all the other questions eventually if they did: the break-in, the journal, the snooping in general, Joe's close call... invading Mariel's personal space. It probably wasn't worth it at this point, monsters in the forest or not.

Joe wandered the shelves, looking across all the book titles, hoping that lightning might strike twice. No secret journals this time, Joe just wanted answers. All the books here had historical value. Texts relevant to the history of the house and William's time, collector's editions that had been acquired over the years and too precious to sell, the occasional random book that occupied space simply because Mariel enjoyed it. Nothing about creatures or mysteries or the unknown. Definitely nothing about the thing in the park.

Ren paced, stirring a cup of tea absentmindedly. "What's a Swinton, anyway?"

"I don't think Swinton is a what so much as a who."

"That's not any more reassuring."

"Than what?" Joe stopped her own search to look at Ren, not following the line of thinking at all.

"What or who, the idea of a forest of Swinton, or a forest *full of* Swintons, sounds forboding."

Joe shuddered a little. "You haven't even seen that thing yet."

Ren stood quietly, considering her response. "So, let's go see it."

Joe dropped the book she'd been holding. "What?"

Ren moved to her, taking her by the hand. "We know better this time. I'll keep you safe."

Joe retracted; she did not share Ren's confidence. "But who will keep *you* safe?"

A smile flashed across her mouth. "You will."

"Ren, I don't think this is a good idea. Don't you remember how worried you were last night?"

"We're better prepared this time."

Joe's eyebrows shot up, compacting her forehead into her hairline. Of all the questions she wanted to ask, none of them seemed to capture the situation as much as the look she was already wearing.

"It's going to be fine, Joe."

"You don't know that."

"No, not until I've had a chance to prove it."

Joe wrung her fingers together while her brain worried behind her eyes. She didn't know how close to death she had actually been, nor did she know if it was the real thing, or just another close call, and she'd wake up and have to start all over again. She didn't want to start over for so many reasons, but especially because it would put Ren in charge of her rehabilitation. That sounded incredibly dangerous.

"What about Tau? Aren't we expecting him?"

Ren pursed her lips, and then shrugged. "I guess he misses out then."

"But we could be followed!"

"Then we'll be extra careful, Joe. What is wrong?"

Her eyes glittered as her fear rose to the surface. "What do you think is wrong, Ren? Think about it. Think about how worried you were just last night – and this morning – and now you are gung ho to send us right back in there together. What if we don't come back from this? What if this is our last chance? Is this how you want to go out?"

Ren took Joe's fingers, lacing them into her

own. "I don't know what's going to happen. I don't know what is waiting for us. What I do know is that there is something bad happening all around us and it's not going to sort itself out." She looked into Joe's eyes, seeing the tears that rimmed them and looked away, afraid she'd follow suit and give up if she lingered. "We will be very careful. And we will not do whatever you did to upset it."

Joe cracked a smile, nodding gently. "Fine, but if it looks like we're doomed, I'm going to murder you first."

Ren shrugged, still holding Joe's hands.

"Good, because I don't want to be the odd one out."

* * * *

Ren and Joe worked their way casually up the path through the woods, Joe leading the way, but only by process of guiding Ren by clutched elbow. Ren occasionally smirked imaging the two of them not much more capable than Shaggy and Scooby, though she wasn't at this moment sure who was who.

They had made their way across the better part of Marysville on foot today, making sure they were not followed. Ducking through shops, taking random buses, and at one point, leaping over, or in Ren's case: into, a small but surprisingly deep brook as they entered the forest.

The element of surprise was lost as Ren sloshed half a step behind Joe, who was trying hard to remain calm as she dug her fingers harder into Ren's arm the further along they travelled.

"I need that arm to stay in one piece, Joe," The tension released for a moment, but returned the moment the leaves flicked in the trees. "Are we there yet?"

This time, Joe meant to squeeze. "I don't know how you can be making jokes at a time like this."

"It's a coping mechanism. If I don't keep levity, I'll realize how terrifying the situation is."

"Well, if you're going to freak out, you better do it now." She pointed to the slight bend in the path where it opened up. Ren could see the fountain bubbling. It almost looked like a fairy tale, the way the fountain was hidden among the trees. "We're here."

Ren took a couple of steps forward into the square. She took a calming breath, reminding herself to be on guard, but appear as non-threatening as possible. Joe held tight for the first couple of paces, but fell behind, the weight of her fear bearing down on her.

Ren wandered, staying close to the fountain at the center. She turned back to Joe, who looked pale and subconsciously rubbed her chest in a slow circle, as if she could feel it returning. When Joe made eye contact, she pointed beyond the fountain. Ren's eyes moved to the end of Joe's invisible arrow and saw it: the time capsule. She swung her foot forward, but she hesitated. Her foot slowly returned to its place beneath her and she waited for a moment. Reaching out, she held a hand splayed, reaching, pawing at the air as she reached back for Joe. Joe again hesitated, and then joined her sister at the center of the crossroads. Together, they sat on the edge of the fountain, hands clasped in a white-knuckle double fist.

Ren licked her lips, swallowed and tried to choose her words carefully to call the creature.

"H-hello?" She waited, happy that they were both off their feet. It was easier to keep her legs from shaking if they weren't supporting her. "Look, we just want to talk."

"Why have you come back?" No one appeared to claim the disembodied voice, but from the first whisper, every muscle in Joe's body tensed, quivering violently. Ren was interested, but focused her worry on protecting Joe and getting some answers.

"I don't know who you think we are, but we're not them." She caressed Joe's fingers, which had gone white with the force of squeezing against Ren's fingers. Ren wanted to step out, to try to find the voice, but even sitting up straighter caused a panic in Joe that held her to the edge of the fountain.

"You are here to take."

The voice flowed through the courtyard, whirling around them as if it were able to go wherever it pleased. Something completely ethereal, but it could apparate and cause extreme physical harm. It made Ren realize that they were no longer part of the world she thought they were a part of. She continued to try to be a part of that ordinary world – the one she left behind – but things kept pointing back to the fact that she would never truly belong there again. Nothing made that more apparent than the fact that she was sitting on a fountain having a conversation with a voice that didn't have a body.

Ren patted Joe's hands, placing them on Joe's lap before boosting herself off the edge of the fountain. There was a sound of protest from Joe, but Ren simply smiled and carried forward with her plan. A plan that, like the voice around her, lacked a body or any sort of substance in general.

"My name is Ren. This is Joe. We're from Delaney House and we need to know if you are keeping something of ours from us. We need it back."

For a long moment, even the wind had stopped. Ren thought that maybe she had overstepped her bounds. Maybe the creature had no idea who the Delaneys were and this had confused it. She listened and waited for a response. Nothing came. She turned back to Joe, who was visibly shaken and staring beyond Ren's shoulder.

At that moment, she realized that she was

Shaggy.

She turned and all at once, her body dragged her back to the lip of the fountain. The creature had appeared far too close for comfort, with barely enough space to slip a breeze between them. Ren immediately felt the cold chill emanating from it. It was a creeping cold, like dry ice. The kind of cold that doesn't just exist; it slithers and crawls.

Ren put a hand out, holding Joe, knowing it was taking everything in the poor girl's soul to keep from running scared. But this was what they came here to find.

It stared at them, into them. It looked almost human, as if it had once been. But it didn't move like a human at all. It moved its head at odd angles, twisting its neck and body instead of just flicking its eyes in a new direction. Its arms floated gently at its sides, as if it were moving through water. Its whole body had a sense of floating, beyond the fact that it was actually floating there in front of them. Its hair and tendrils and tattered remnants of cloth all seemed to float aimlessly as if gravity had no effect on it.

"You know nothing of what you ask. It is not

yours."

When it spoke, nothing moved. Its lips never parted, its chest didn't rise or fall. Its eyes didn't even appear to glimmer, showing that it was transmitting a psychic message just for them. It was as if someone was operating it from behind a curtain. That thought circled, and then came to roost again in Ren's brain. It seemed like a very good way to keep everything safe and secure.

She peered around the park, looking for any indication that it was just a projection, or a hologram, or something. Her eyes moved past Joe's who gave her a curious look, as if she couldn't believe Ren had found something more interesting than this creature. Ren could only wink and hope Joe understood.

Ren stood up again, stepping forward, feeling the cold drip off it. She ignored the warnings her body tried to provide and reached out, expecting her hand to pass through it.

It did not.

Way to go, Shaggy.

It cocked its head, giving her the curious look of a dog that didn't understand its master, then repeated Ren's motion, its fingers lighting on her chest. Immediately, Ren felt the cold shock her body. All of her functions ceased for a long moment. And when she thought the worst was over, it placed its full hand onto her chest, the sensation doubling as it forced its way into her system.

Ren realized that she must be getting the worst of it for her offense, because there was no way she would make it back to Delaney House the way she felt at this moment – let alone grab a pizza on the way. Somewhere behind her, Joe let out a strangled cry and Ren realized that it couldn't end here.

"Enough." Her demand was feeble, soft. She had willed it to slip from her lips and even she barely heard it. She said it again, trying to be more forceful, but the air was heavy in her lungs. It moved slowly and without force. The white face in front of her remained impassive and uncaring. Ren did not want to die. Not here, certainly not again. She had been lucky the last time.

Her hands came up, one closing around the fingers on her chest, the other reaching out. She peeled the frozen digits from her bluing flesh and with her other hand, she shoved.

"Enough!"

It came clear and strong this time, and for a moment, she thought the warmth would return to her, but that was momentary. She collapsed to her knees on the stones, holding herself, shuddering in the cold that burned within her. Joe rushed to her side, the words that might have been spoken any other time were only a whimper that forced its way through tears.

Ren reached out, grasping Joe's hand and wanting to speak. She wanted to say all sorts of things. She wanted to be witty and inspiring and encouraging. She wanted to ease the moment for both of them, but the burning cold within her made her whole body shake and complicated the act of providing inspiration.

"I guess we'll see what happens," She held Joe, and didn't want to leave, but it was getting harder to keep her eyes open. Her body was getting colder and her thoughts seemed to be slowing down. It was coming soon. It wouldn't be a quick surprise this time. It was going to come on like an old movie: slow, familiar, with a gradual build to the finale.

"You are not like most who come here."

Ren tried to open her eyes. Something had changed in its tone. It sounded curious, almost apologetic. Her muscles wouldn't obey her any longer. She was doubled over, ready to collapse. She could feel hands guiding her onto her side, then her back. She assumed it was Joe. When she managed to peek through the tiny slits that were all that remained of her vision, she saw only the thing. She felt it place a hand on her chest again and she rattled out a cough. At any other time in her life, it would have been a scream, long and loud, but it was too close to the end now, and the cough was all the remained of her defiant nature.

She felt her energy wane, and with it, the cold. It was like she could feel her whole body warming up. It took a moment to realize, but that was exactly what was happening. She could feel her extremities again, the blood working its way through her body, feeling hotter and thicker than ever before.

She gasped, her body dragging her upright. Her eyes opened and before she could do anything, her wind was taken away again as Joe tackled her. She continued to cry, but Ren could tell these were happy, delighted tears. It was the steel grip Joe held her with that worried her.

Over Joe's shoulder, she saw the creature staring down at them, observing this moment with casual curiosity. Ren looked up as she hugged Joe.

"Thank you."

It made no move to communicate compassion or sympathy. It seemed just as impassive as when it was trying to kill her. But something in the air had certainly changed. The energy itself felt different.

"It would be wasteful to remove you from this place. Your strength can do much good here."

FOURTEEN

Weary and exhausted didn't come close to how they both felt as they leaned against each other, hardly noticing the jostles as they rode around on Marysville's public transit. For one low price, the bus system would take them anywhere, and let them ride as long as the shuttle was running, for no additional fee. Ren and Joe bobbed along as the bus shimmied around corners, stopping every so many blocks to pick up or drop off. No one paid them much mind as they slipped in and out the fog they shared, trying to force their brains to understand everything that had been passed along to them in such a short time.

After it had revived Ren, the creature revealed itself as a she, not an it. She, like Mariel, was a den mother. The two not only shared the common bond of surrogate motherhood, but also that of an unnaturally long history. So long in this case, that she did not actually remember where she came from when she and Mariel first crossed paths. Mariel was fortunate enough to find the den mother in a complacent mood and struck a bargain.

Mariel called her new friend Mother Wight, and neither Ren nor Joe wanted to point out the folklore that Mariel had borrowed that name from. Really, she could have borrowed from any number of fairytales and it didn't matter as long as Mother Wight herself never found out what it meant. That didn't seem to be a concern. Mother and her brood had no desire to be part of any society but their own. The city had been encroaching on their hunting ground for some time, and when their territory became threatened, they began attacking. That's when the stories began: tales of boogeymen and evil spirits coming in with the fog, attacking the townsfolk. Mariel went out, primarily defenseless, into a heavy fog, when they were known to attack. That was when she met Mother and her brood, stuffing themselves on what remained of a horse they had brought down.

Mariel showed no fear and proceeded to try to communicate. It took time, but Mariel and Mother were able to find a common ground for language. They began a discussion that started as a parlay and turned into an agreement based on the bonds of friendship, as absurd as this one might be. Mariel led them into a section of forest that had been tabled for some future city development. She showed them the boundaries and, on her own authority, gave them the forest. Later, she would set out to turn the forest into a nature preserve, protecting much more than this group of creatures. They in turn kept to the forest, finding ways to mask their existence, and learning to coexist with the less-troublesome humans.

It wasn't until much later that Mariel came to Mother with the dagger. Mother had no real understanding of emotion, making her completely useless in the line of questions Ren and Joe had for her as they sought further clues to what the dagger was and why it was so important.

Mother could only tell them that it had been left under her protection and they were the first to try to claim it. But they had not been the only ones in the forest recently.

"She never even bothered apologizing for trying to kill me," Joe spoke softly, hoping no one else on the bus was eager to eavesdrop. "Or you."

"I don't think she understands what being sorry is."

"Well she should learn," Joe was interrupted with a yawn. "You could teach her."

Ren scoffed. "Maybe some other time. I am much more worried about whatever else is going on."

Joe shuddered. Mother had told them about other beings in the forest – she had used the word *beings* specifically, not *humans*. She had kept her distance, keeping guard over her promise to Mariel, but other members of her den started disappearing. It was the first time either Ren or Joe saw her express anything that resembled emotion, and it was not anything they liked experiencing. Ren took it on a guess that wights had the emotional range of an animal, which meant a scale of extremes. She could see it as Mother tried to tell them about her missing brood. Cold rage poured out of her; she seethed with sorrow and anger. Worse was that no matter how she tried to convey it, she didn't seem to know how to express her fear. She could only rage at the unknown, even to her two new allies.

They looked around the bus again before Joe continued. "You think someone is hunting them? But who?"

"And how? Even if they don't have Mother's abilities, they can't be easy to bring down." Though Ren was relieved that only Mother had her abilities. Only she had been around long enough to attain them. Mother had explained that younger wights could mask themselves, camouflaging themselves in their environment, and hiding in shadows. They hunted with the speed and efficiency of predatory kings and once they had your scent, they could track you forever. But whatever was hunting the wights didn't leave a trail. It was silent, invisible and exceptionally dangerous.

"Do you think Tau's mystery men have anything to do with it?"

Ren nodded. She would almost bet that Tau and Eunice Abernathy were both tied to this… somehow. She didn't understand how everything fit together, but Ren had the distinct feeling that it was all coming to a head, and she and Joe were already caught right in the middle.

They got off at the last stop in Old Town just after midnight. Like their last hike back from the shopping district, they were weary, muscles aching. Unlike last time, there was nothing to be happy about. As the days wore on, the news only got worse. Thieves, and vendettas, now folklore and who knows what else come to roost in their anonymous little lives. They dragged along the sidewalks, arms around each other keeping one another on their feet.

Silently they walked, the dark house loping into view. Ren wished to herself for it all just to be over. She wanted Mariel and Colette to be waiting at home for them, to have all the answers they'd been seeking and to put an end to all this chaos once and for all.

When that didn't happen, she closed her eyes and held tighter to Joe as they shuffled closer to home.

* * * *

Ren sat at the end of the couch, her limbs strewn in uncomfortable looking positions, but she gave them no mind. A pot of tea cooled on the table in the common room, steam drifting into the air. Joe's deep breathing was the only sound in the room, and even that was mostly ignored by Ren, her thoughts operating overtime. There had to be a way this all fit together. One that made sense.

As if anything makes sense around here.

It was as fair a point as it was a jab. Ren fought the bitterness that was welling, the anger she felt against Mariel. It wasn't fair that they were stuck in the middle of a situation that was not theirs to begin with. Mariel had left them with nothing. There had been no warnings, and neither of them was answering their phone.

Everything had been left to their own devices. Why had Mariel not warned anyone that this might be coming? Certainly, if she knew to hide the dagger, then she knew well enough that there was some sort of danger – *which they all might be in.* How could Mariel play at such a risk?

Ren sat up and poured a cup of tea, standing up to pace the room. She walked the length twice more, retracing steps both physical and mental as she tried to find that elusive fragment that fit everything together. She moved up and down the floors, seeing the paths where foot traffic had worn things down. Paths moved everywhere: from room to room, across in distinctive patterns to certain shelves, even some places at the table saw more traffic than others. But only one door lacked regular foot traffic. Only one door had ever been spoken of in hushed tones, and she walked toward it now.

In a dozen steps she found herself standing in front of that great wood door, one that she had only stepped beyond once. Mariel's office was probably locked whenever she was not in it – probably sometimes when she was – and it would have to be broken into. She would explain herself later; she didn't need anything but probable cause right now. It was an old door; maybe she could just force the lock.

Maybe you've seen too many movies.

She slipped her fingers around the knob, pressing her shoulder to the door. She gave the knob a firm abrupt twist and was surprised to find that the door simply opened. She pulled on the door to brace herself and keep her from falling into the room. Such a mess would only set them back further, and right now, this was the only good sign they'd had. Or was it such a good sign?

Perhaps Mariel left the door unlocked in the event that they needed to get in here. Then either she or Joe would try, finding it unlocked. Had she anticipated this, or just anticipated a need?

Ren shook her head, she could ask these questions later.

She looked into the room, into the organized chaos that Mariel dwelled in. This was another in a theme, and she had no idea where to begin the search here either. She sat down at Mariel's desk and took in the room. She repeated the phrase to herself: organized chaos. That's exactly what this room was. While everything was in piles and stacks and stuffed into shelves, it was all Mariel's way of putting things into groups, keeping it all together. Now, Ren just had to figure out what mattered and what didn't.

She started with the desk itself, figuring that

anything that meant something to Mariel would be kept close by. In one drawer, she found nothing but business cards. Ren shuffled through them, looking for a name that might stick out, but none did. The next drawer down: ledgers. Stacks of black faux leather ledgers – and one brown one – filled the drawer end to end. She wondered how many of them were full, and how many Mariel might have bought just for consistency. She furrowed her brow at the brown one and it's faded faux velour exterior, wondering if this occurred before purchasing the lot of black ledgers, or if maybe she felt a need to change for a moment, realizing the error of her ways and going back to her professional consistency.

The rest of the drawers revealed little more than Mariel's organizational ability. A drawer for her pens and other tools: scissors, a ruler, an assortment of paper clips, sticky notes, and a stapler. A drawer full of newspaper clippings, commendations, small plaques and other memorabilia Ren was certain came from charity events that Delaney House had been a participant in.

She flipped through the clippings with interest, taking in each one, looking for a clue, but all she gained an insight on was that Mariel was invested in making this place a staple of the community. She smiled inwardly; there was no reason it shouldn't be. But there was nothing in the drawer that would give her any clues to what she was at the center of.

Her mind continued to peck at her, sending her back to the ledgers. She pulled them out, flipping through them one at a time. Mariel had kept track of dates and details for everything acquired since she had started amassing her collection. She made mention of purchases versus donations, previous ownership, anything that she thought might be worth noting.

She flipped through a handful of black books before deciding that she should look in the odd one out. It called to her that someone like Mariel, so precise and particular in her ways, would have one book that did not match the others – especially when there were at least a dozen in the other variety. She flipped through noticing the same penmanship, the same collection of details. She flipped the pages faster, looking for that one item out of place that would be a clue, but it didn't seem to be there. She flipped backward through the book, paranoid that she might have missed something. It was a ledger, nothing more. The dates didn't share the same consistency as with the other ledgers, but perhaps this was a special collection. Ren stopped on a random page and there it was: the clue had been right before her eyes from the beginning.

The organization was still the same, but the details were completely different. It took Ren a couple of pages before she realized she was reading a shorthand journal of Mariel's private life.

She turned one page after another, trying to translate the phrases, not certain what most of them meant. She decided it would be prudent to work from the end, where she had the most knowledge. She flipped to the last page that contained Mariel's unmistakable handwriting on it and stared at the first entry at the top:

The Flower: Full recovery.

It was like being taken back to her old life all at once. Her mother had always called Ren – Florence – her little flower. It had been a pun that she and her mother shared, with her mother always teasing Ren about blossoming into a woman. She wished her mother were still here, maybe she could help her laugh at the way she had been plucked from her old life and placed in this one.

She shook it off, trying to remind herself that there was something she was looking for, but the words pulled her back in again. They might not mean a lot to many people, but to anyone who might access it – especially Ren at this moment – it spoke volumes. To anyone in this house, who had gone through the same process, it meant everything. And it meant more to her that Mariel had bothered to write it down. But the next entry pushed Ren back into bewilderment:

The Queen is restless. Needs to be moved.

The Queen? Who is she? Ren wondered if this was the reason that they had left so abruptly. Something to do with a queen, or *The* Queen, as it was written. But who and what kind of queen was she?

She began to flip through the pages, looking at entries, most of them progress points and updates on members of the house, not just the four here, but all of them. And all of them had secret code names, meaning Mariel had reason to protect each of them from something out there. As she continued to flip the pages, she felt more than heard someone step through the threshold. She could feel their eyes on her. Certain that Joe was awake and wanting to know what she was doing, Ren turned and felt the shock of surprise as she looked up into Tau's curious face.

"Find something?"

"What are you doing? I thought we had a strict no-breaking-no-entering understanding."

"What are you reading?"

Ren stood up and shoved him back against the door. "You aren't supposed to be here. I will fill you in later, now leave."

He smiled and Ren saw his teeth. Things were suddenly very out of her control. He had broken in; he didn't seem concerned at all – and where was Joe?

Their eyes met and his smile got bigger. He held his hand out, palm up.

"You're getting it now. This is my game. Hand it over."

She grit her teeth and hesitated, but she

slapped the book down into his hand. Inwardly, she prayed he had no idea what he was looking at. She could tell by the look on his face as he turned page to page that he didn't. He looked up at her after a handful of pages.

"What the hell is this?"

"I don't know yet, but it seemed important. It's different from the other ones."

He threw the book at the desk. "I don't have time for this! Where is the knife? I know you're close to getting it."

Her surprise betrayed her. She knew exactly where he stood now, with his cheshire grin as he stepped in so close, all she could see were his glaring eyes.

"You know where it is, don't you? Tell me. It'll be that much easier for both of us."

"I'm not telling you anything. Not until I know the whole story."

"You'll tell me everything, or poor little Joe – "

She didn't even let him finish. Ren jabbed him hard in the stomach, pitching him over and darted out into the living room. It was empty. No sign of a struggle, but no sign of Joe. Something had happened. Ren turned on her heel, eyes shooting daggers into him as he caught his breath, his cough turning to laughter, shallow and confident.

"She's fine. *For now.* See for yourself."

He pointed at the window and she crossed the room, leaning over the couch to see out into the front yard. Even in the darkness, she could make out Joe's pale skin shining in the glow from the streetlights. She looked weak, tired. She also looked terrified. She was suspended between two—

Ren gasped. She was being held in place by monsters. Glistening black creatures that towered over Joe. They were twisted and strange, shuffling back and forth, but bore a strange resemblance to Mother Wight. Ren shook her head. Was this Mother's missing brood? If so, what had happened to them?

"I am sure you recognize them, or at least the resemblance. I'd like to tell you we have an army of them, but that's simply not the case. It took a lot of trial and error to transform them into these perfect soldiers. Lots of experimentation; *lots* of sacrifices."

Ren stared back at Tau, horrified by his pride in this horror. She opened her mouth to say something, but nothing would come, no matter how she tried to force it.

"Still, what they lack in numbers, they make up for in skill. They're perfectly silent – as you can tell. They were here and gone and you never noticed. I'll even just tell you: they're blind. They don't rely on sight at all. But don't get hopeful: they're the perfect bloodhounds. There is no escaping them, and right now, I am the only thing keeping them from tearing your little friend apart and drinking her dry."

Ren shot up, her arms clenched, ready for the fight he was edging toward, but he held up a hand.

"We don't care about you, or her. We want the knife."

Her jaw tightened and she begged her tears to stay hidden. She would address them later. "I don't have it."

He smiled, raising an eyebrow as if he knew better. "You can get it. You're resourceful. Besides, Joe's life depends on it. You wouldn't let her down, would you?"

He stepped around her, walking toward the door.

"I think two days is fitting, don't you? Obviously, the sooner you deliver it, the better shape she'll be in, but I wouldn't drag it out till the last minute."

Her jaw was set, she couldn't even look at him for fear what she might do that would jeopardize Joe.

"What about Panya, *your* sister? Or was that just a story?"

"Oh no, she's real. She is with our family, safe and sound. She has no idea where I am."

She turned toward him, and felt her body betraying her under the weight of the moment. Hate burned in her eyes, emphasized by the tears that boiled over. Her fists shook and her lips quivered, she wanted to tear him limb from limb where he stood smirking at her.

"Don't keep us waiting, but don't show up without the knife."

"Where am I supposed to find you?"

"I'm sure you can figure it out; you were so close last time."

All she could do was stare as he walked out

the door and spoke something to Joe. Ren stood on quaking limbs as Joe looked up at her. Her eyes were pleading, and she shook her head almost imperceptibly.

Please don't, Joe's eyes begged. But please don't what? Don't follow? Don't try to save her? Don't give them the knife?

She clenched her hands tight against her chest as she watched them slowly drag her away, Joe's weakened muscles straining with no impact on her captors. She watched until they dissolved into the darkness, then she watched longer, standing at the window, every muscle quaking with anger. She never noticed that she had dug wounds into her own palms with her fingernails, and when she finally did, they were the least of her worries.

She had to get the knife, get Joe, and get revenge.

FIFTEEN

The moment it was decided, Ren collapsed. She buckled under the weight of tears and conflict and anger all roiling inside her, demanding to be felt. She took a minute; let the pressure ease, and then stowed the rest back inside. She wanted to forget everything except the one goal: get Joe back. She marched out into the dark, travelling the long quiet roads alone, her boot heels echoing off the buildings as she walked.

The entire time, she tried to convince herself that this part wasn't necessary. That it was very much the opposite of a safe plan, but Ren was looking for some kind of advantage and this seemed to be the only one available to her. She knew what Mariel would say. Everyone would say the same thing, really. And she completely agreed, but she also stopped caring the minute Tau stepped into the office tonight. He had drawn a line and she was primed to destroy everything on his side of it.

She strode into Swinton Woods, hardly certain of any particular direction she was going in, but somehow she found her way to the fountain anyhow. She told herself the hand of Fate was guiding her, but she hardly believed it. It was the slow realization of what she intended to do. She didn't want to be alone in this decision, but deep down she knew this was a solo operation.

"Mother!"

She called out and turned around on the stones, waiting for her to appear. A mist was drifting slowly down the hill, but hardly in any particular direction. Ren thought by the chill in the air that she might be coming, but a moment later it became clear that the chill was her adrenaline wearing down combined with an actual atmospheric chill in the air.

"Mother! You need to give it to me."

She waited again, expecting at least a simple

"no", but none came. Mother was either sleeping it off in the deepest of dreams, or she was watching, intent on keeping the knife safe. Ren clenched her jaw and stepped off the path into the thick of the forest. She wasn't sure where to begin looking, but she knew she had to try. Joe was depending on her.

If Joe's still alive…

She stopped midstride. Her heart felt like a stone at the thought and she promised not to utter such a terrible thing ever again, not even in the privacy of her own mind; or perhaps especially not there.

The further off the path she wandered, the stranger the forest seemed. Perhaps not strange, but wild. It grew like it had never seen the Age of Man. The trees were thick and timeless, and she was almost sure that she had stumbled into another land. Certainly someone would have noticed these trees growing in the middle of the city. But here they stood. Leaves and branches and thick undergrowth hampered her stride, making her consider her steps more carefully. As she continued on, she looked around and realized there was no way out of here. Every direction looked the same, all of them seeming to head deeper into the woods.

I guess the only way out is through. Let's hope that's true.

The longer she travelled; she started to feel the weight and aggression leaving her. She was mesmerized by the woods; enchanted by them and giving in to their overwhelming calm. It occurred to her that this might be part of how the wights hunted, that right now they could be hunting her. Part of her was surprisingly okay with it.

We're all part of the life cycle, after all. The dirt and the plants and the bugs and the small creatures and the big creatures and me…

And then she remembered, though a growing majority of her brain didn't care so much, that she was not at the top of the food chain in this part of the woods. She continued to move through the dark, able to catch a glimmer here and there to keep her from running face first into a tree. She carried on, not even sure how long she'd been out there, when she came to a clearing.

The clearing had a soft green bed of growth,

nothing overgrown, nothing gnarled and tangled. Just a perfectly open patch of woods where the grass was soft beneath her feet and starlight shone down from above her. In the center of the clearing stood a squat object. As she approached, Ren had a peculiar sense of dread, as if this was one a great tree, and now there was only a stump. But as she grew closer to the object, she felt relief: no missing trees, but there was a long abandoned chest at her feet.

Her heart leapt, as she knelt and examined the chest. It was wood, with old metal trim. She placed extra emphasis on the word old. All of the trim was long rusted and eaten away in places. The lock on the front was rusted into place; she couldn't get it to budge at all. The wood was warped and bent and almost felt rotten. She pulled at the box; it felt fused to the forest floor. After all this time, it might have done exactly that. There was no way to get it out of the forest if she couldn't even pick it up. And if she couldn't get it out of the forest, she'd never get it open.

She clenched her teeth and stood up, frustrated at nature's lack of cooperation, and kicked the trunk – surprised to feel it crumple under her boot. She put her foot right through everything but the metal frame and got caught up in it, tripping over her good fortune.

Ren scrambled forward on her hands and knees, pawing through the spongy old wood, feeling for the contents of the box, and hoping the same fate had not befallen them. She could feel the small bugs and worms that had been living within the walls of the trunk skittering over her hand as she dug through the remains, huffing frantically as she tried to find something – anything.

She continued until she was certain she had sifted through the entire mess that was once a chest. Whatever was here had been moved long ago. She felt disappointment blanketing her. She could not leave empty handed. She needed a new lead; she couldn't just give up.

Maybe I haven't looked hard enough. These woods go on forever and –

As she stood up and turned, Ren found that she was surrounded. Seven wights, each as tall and lean as Mother, but each with a much more aggressive aura than hers. Maybe she was onto something after all. It also occurred to her that she might not be leaving the woods tonight. Or at all.

She stood in place, turning slowly as she addressed them. Her hands were out at her sides; fingers splayed to show her hands were empty.

"I'm not sure if you understand me as well as Mother, but I need that knife." They were impassive, not even bothering to consider her with curiosity. "If I don't find it, someone will die."

"If you do find it, someone will die." Ren whirled at the sound of Mother, but couldn't see her. Everywhere she turned, it was one of seven interchangeable faces, each as cold and expressionless as the last. Her fingers clenched into fists as she looked up into the trees.

"So you want me to just abandon her? No! Give it to me."

"We cannot." The voice moved around her. "We made a pact."

"They're going to kill her!"

"You intend to kill them. I do not see the difference."

"I'm trying to save her!" Ren was quaking,

every muscle in her body wanting to scream out at them, to make them understand. Mother appeared in a swirl of arctic mist. Like her brood, she showed no reaction. Unlike her kin, she did seem to regard Ren with curiosity – or maybe, Ren thought, it could even be concern.

"If you were to fail, they would possess the knife, and this cannot happen."

"What is the big deal with this knife?" She was on the verge of collapse, trying to have a conversation with an otherworldly being about compassion and it was going about as well as one might expect. She was at her wit's end. "If I'm going to give up, you had better have a really good reason."

"The knife is at the center of all misery in the Delaney House."

Ren shook her head slowly, stumbling over her words as she tried to ask the right question. "What do you mean 'all misery'?"

"William cursed himself by taking the knife. Mariel cursed herself by keeping the knife. All of you are cursed because she knows it is here and she wants it."

Ren swallowed. "You mean Eunice

Abernathy." The cold silence that followed was more than enough confirmation and she nodded. Mother knew that name, or she would have said something. "Why does she want it so badly?"

"We only know that it is powerful, and she has tried many times to possess it. She has destroyed many who have stood in her way. It cannot fall into her hands."

"She took members from your den, didn't she?" For the briefest of instants, there was something on Mother Wight's face. A wince perhaps, some twinge of pain. It was enough to know that she had the one thing that might have saved them, but she couldn't do anything about it. When Ren spoke again, her voice was soft, understanding, but resolved just the same. "I can't let anything happen to Joe."

She looked from Mother to the other seven in the circle around her. No one moved. It occurred to her that someone might mistake them for horrifying statues if they were to ever set foot in this part of the woods. Of course, they'd also have to live to tell anyone after the discovery.

"If you're not going to give me the knife,

then give me something, anything." She took a deep breath and her shoulders slumped. "I need help. Please. I'm begging you."

"What she did to them, my children, they can never come home. They are not our brood any longer. But they are still our kind." She hunched over, staring intently, as if sizing Ren up. "The change has slowed them. They are clumsy and blind."

Ren decided not to correct her. They didn't appear to be clumsy, even if they were blind. They looked meaner and more dangerous than the group she was currently with.

"They are tainted, hardly more than beasts now." Mother gave no warning, but reached out and grabbed Ren by the shoulders.

At first it was the shock of surprise that clutched at her, then it was the burning cold from Mother's touch. The sensation spread and she wanted to speak up, but the burning cold travelled down her extremities and flowed back up into her heart and her brain. She fought the pain as best she could; trying to remind herself that it wasn't the same terrible experience as the first time Mother had put a hand on her.

"They will try to hunt you by your blood, but they will not find you now."

And then her vision faded. Ren was certain that she had passed out, but it was actually her vision failing. She was amazed how quickly her hearing picked up on things when she suddenly couldn't see. Even more amazing was the fact that none of the wights seemed to make any noise at all. They didn't breathe, didn't shift their weight, nothing. They were fearless, mighty, killing machines.

...*That kind of adopted you. Consider yourself lucky.*

She tried to look in the direction of Mother Wight, unable to tell in the dark if her vision was returning at all.

"I'm sorry about your brood."

There was a long silence. "I am... sorry about yours. Find her."

"I'm going to."

She sat down in the grass and listened to the absolute absence of nature. She could hear the breeze in the treetops, but that was it. The animals were either sleeping, or too afraid to venture into this part of the woods. Ren opted for the latter of the two.

As her vision returned, she could see the faint outlines of the trees and the stars overhead. She was alone in the clearing and she realized that she had no idea how long after she spoke to Mother that they had left. She really hoped that whatever Mother had done to her would give her the upper hand. She didn't feel the confidence she wanted to as she got to her feet. Her extremities burned like frostbite, and she couldn't feel most of her body, as it if the whole thing was numb from the cold.

"Some upper hand… I'm a meat popsicle."

SIXTEEN

In the early hours, while stars still spun in the darkness over head, and morning was still deciding if it should bother getting up, Ren considered the options available to her. She considered William Delaney's cavalry sword. She didn't know if it was sharp, but it was metal and had a pointy end, which could probably be considered an advantage. She could break into a sporting goods store, or a gun shop. It was certainly adding another level of risk to the situation, but a gun might be just the thing to even the odds. She also considered the police, the military, and borrowing a number of religious tools from one of the many churches in the area.

She weighed her options as she walked,

balancing pros against cons, considering any long-term ramifications of joining the criminal element in order to save Joe. In the end, she found herself pondering right up to the rusty old fence line that separated her from the quarry.

She stared into the dark grounds, remembering that she followed Tau up to this point once before. She believed that this was what he was hinting at, but she hadn't intended to come here yet. Something inside her pulled her to this spot, even when she considered turning back for something that might help. Was Joe in there? She held the chain link fence, threading her fingers through the holes as she closed her eyes.

Take a deep breath, Ren.

She heard Colette's voice and followed the instructions. Her lungs inflated and she tried to ignore the strange sensations of her numb muscles. She exhaled and paused, then repeated the process. She could feel the world slip away slightly after a handful of breaths. It could have been the loss of her tactile senses that heightened everything, or her abilities had gotten stronger, but in the dead cold of her chest, she felt an ember of warmth. A small glow reached out from within her, searching outward.

Like last time, it started out everywhere, reaching outward and pushing into the world like psychic feelers. She had no idea how far she was pushing with it, or if any of her sisters could feel it, but slowly, she could feel it separate into specific directions. There were two very strong points tugging at her, each one felt like they were toward opposite horizons. The other houses, she mused. She could feel sisters she hadn't even met yet. But they weren't the ones she was looking for.

She tried to rein it in. She thought about Joe. Joe: with her bright eyes and their mischievous glint. The way the corners of her mouth seemed permanently curled, ready to snap into an infectious smile at any moment. She felt the glowing warmth inside her searching outward; looking for the girl that sent sparks down Ren's spine with every giggle, every touch of their fingers. She spun her brain out into the universe like a lure, trying to hook the soul entwined with her own.

It was like a punch to the sternum. The

sensation within her snapped down to a single point and she cried out, gasping. Her eyes wide, she searched the darkness looking for the point at the end of the line between them. She couldn't see the line, or much at all in the darkness, but she remembered a structure deep in the quarry. Joe was there, and she could sense that things were not going well.

Her brain still wanted her to turn around and find something to defend herself with, but the urgency would not be denied. She needed to trust her intuition. She needed to save Joe.

...*Or die trying.*

Of course, there was still the hope that she couldn't actually die, but she wasn't keen on finding out.

She wandered down the fence line, looking for the simplest – and quietest – way in. She found it about half a block further than when she had given up looking for Tau last time. The chain links were separated from the support pipe, but placed in such a way that they still appeared secure. It was a deliberate placement, and it told Ren she was on the right trail. She crept through the fence and slowly navigated her way down the first ledge she came to, moving further into the stone yard.

Though the signage on the fence line suggested an industrial park, there was no park to it. It was a fenced-in property that had been cut away and turned into a quarry. A labyrinthine network of canals cut through the property, providing two levels of traffic for machines and travelers. Ren was glad to be here in the dark. Some of the passages were long and didn't appear to leave a lot of wiggle room, should any large machines come rolling through.

Her eyes were wide, taking in what light they could find. The whole scape seemed almost alien in the pre-morning dark, appearing before her eyes in a scheme of deep blue on black. She wandered, occasionally creeping up the corridor walls where she could find a foothold, hoping to see something of interest. She could feel herself getting closer to her destination, though she could not actually see it yet. The night was shapeless; the building could be right in front of her and she might never know.

Ren had lost all sense of time tonight. It was already late when this began and now, the deep dark blue was giving way to lighter hues, finally pulled the veil from her blind progress. One black shadow loomed ahead of her, and the sensation within her insistently blinked 'you are here'. The closer she came, the more obvious it became that she should probably turn tail and give the army a call.

It appeared to be three stories, maybe taller. The first stories had walls of steel, bolted together and probably set into the ground around it. Above, everything up to the roof appeared to be glass, but nothing showed. It was possible the whole place was dark inside; it was also possible that the windows were all obscured. Ren wandered the perimeter, looking for an entrance.

The main entrance was large and solid like the rest of the ground floor. Two large doors were framed by a track on top and bottom and appeared to slide apart to grant entrance. She could see the deep grooves in the ground, showing all of the traffic in and out. She didn't know the last time anyone had come through here, or if anyone was left inside right now. There was always a possibility she could walk right in. But if anyone was standing guard, she couldn't slip through that doorway undetected.

She continued around the perimeter, hoping for something – a small entrance into the offices, or maybe a window so she could get a look inside. What she found was a choking stench and a definite last resort. Behind the building, a large pipe sent runoff into a stagnant pool. It gurgled and sounded like semi-solid matter colliding with one another as it fell from the pipe. It smelled like something rotten had found something equally awful, and together, they raised an awful, rotting family in this pool. She held her mouth and nose, considering taking a chance with suffocation over smelling it a moment longer. Ren turned to run full tilt in the other direction when she realized, against her better judgment, that this pipeline might be her ticket inside.

She climbed down carefully, straddling the pipe. If she fell in by mistake, she would take her chances with the afterlife, because there would be no washing that stink and shame away. The pipe ran underneath the ground by a few feet, and hovered over the cesspool it emptied into by another handful. Ren carefully lowered herself over the edge of the pipe, holding on for dear life until her feet found solid purchase. She reeled herself inside and was happy to find that she only had to lower her head slightly to navigate the tunnel. Walking was at best an awkward shuffle as she kept her feet to the sides of the curved path, keeping her shoes out of anything slick that she might slip in.

Step by step, Ren moved further into the tunnel, listening to the sound of her own breath growing heavier and more anxious in the choking stench. The darkness pressed in around her the farther she moved from the opening, continuing on one step at a time, her hands pressed against the cool metal walls for support.

She continued to shuffle forward. Whether fifty paces or a hundred and fifty, she never bothered to count. Her focus was on each moment in turn and her anxious shallow breaths as she tried with all her might to fight down the urge to throw up with each continued step. The stench seemed to grow, if that was even possible after what she smelled outside. She made a note to contact someone in the EPA when this was all over.

Ren was certain that she must have passed

under the exterior of the structure by now. But without any indicators, she had no idea how far she was in either direction. It was still dark enough outside that she had lost the opening to the outside world, and apparently dark enough inside that she couldn't see the end of the tunnel. It was a sudden surprise when she realized that she could actually see her hands moving on the rounded walls. The light was faint where she was, but it was enough to give her batteries a jolt. She continued forward, focused on moving as quietly as possible, the tunnel getting lighter as she moved, reflecting an orange glow from somewhere ahead.

As she surged on, the smells changed. The rotten stench combined with a charred smell. Something was definitely burning. She could hear the roar of fire growing and assumed it was the source of light as well. Each new step brought another onslaught of sensory information. Around her, somewhere above or below the roar of the fire, there was a rumbling. It was deep and constant, but she couldn't feel it when her fingers touched the tunnel walls. She could hear run off; that same sickening noise that invited her on this journey also harkened its end, or vice versa. And then came the icing on the cake: a choking swarm of flies here at the end of the line.

Ren covered her mouth and shut her eyes, the swarm so thick they couldn't help but pelt her as she tried to pass through them. The buzz of a multitude of wings was deafening, it seemed to drown out all other noises. She continued to stumble forth, feeling the insects bounce off her. She could only pad blindly forward, forcing her way through the blizzard of pests. She couldn't bring herself to touch the walls again. Putting a hand out in the thick of the insect tornado around her resulted in the soft squish of who knows how many frenzied creatures. To her benefit, Ren's careful shuffling allowed her to kick the wall that signaled the end of the journey, before she actually ran headlong into the oozing mess.

She opened her eyes to slits, noticing that the flies were less congested here. It helped that the grating above her allowed them to move into the open air, but the grating was going to be a problem for a human-sized intruder like herself.

Ren pressed her face up, trying to look

around. All she could see were tall slick piles of refuse, what she assumed was the source of the stench in the first place. While this meant much more deep scrubbing when this was all over, it also meant that she could possibly emerge completely unseen.

She listened carefully, trying to hear above all the ambient sounds that demanded her attention. Beyond the sounds of the fire and the earth and the insects, Ren was almost certain she heard nothing else nearby. Her fingers slid into the spaces in the grate, cringing as those same spaces squished between her fingers and she closed them around the metal. She pushed upward and for what it made in stench and mess, the viscous runoff made an excellent lubricant for the metal grate as Ren lifted and slid it to the side. It moved without so much as a squeak and she was able to settle it with little more than a soft thud before sliding it across and causing a cascade of sick to rush into the hole above her.

It took everything in her power not to scream as the cold ooze weaved through her hair and slid down her neck. She clenched her jaw and shook it off, reminding herself why she was here. She couldn't sense Joe now and tried not to panic. Her surroundings were too dangerous to divert any of her concentration toward their link; she would have to find her the old fashion way.

Her head popped up through the hole carefully, spying around all of the objects around her. She couldn't make out much; the fires making shadows dance as much as the light itself changed from moment to moment. But as she concentrated, she saw nothing that looked like it was standing guard. It was enough of an incentive to try to get out of the hole.

She ignored her brain screaming for her not to touch anything. She didn't come all this way to just give up because she was going to get dirty. So, it was more than just dirty, it was probably a health hazard for anyone who was behind on his or her vaccinations. There might even be some new biological threat being born in this mess as she waded through it, but there was no time to worry about that now. The needs of the many would have to wait.

Ren hoisted herself up, kicking her legs out and rolling onto her back to save herself the misfortune of pressing her face into the runoff around her. She raised herself slowly, peering around the piles that guarded her. She saw nothing new, just the fires and piles of... remains? She didn't want to think about it.

It must be some sort of dumping ground, but whose?

She got to her feet, slipping around the small piles that hid her escape route, and darted to a wall. She clung to it as she got a handle on her surroundings. The ceilings looked much higher here than on the outside. And though it may have appeared to be three stories out there, inside it was one open structure in this part. Catwalks moved here and there overhead, chains and rails hanging in places where other parts of the structure may once have been, but they had come down some time ago. Ahead of her, the building appeared to open up more. Walls seemed to go only as high as necessary in here, as she could see the top of the wall she was leaning against, though she could never reach it to climb up. The wall, and what she assumed was it's adjoining room, had to be fourteen feet tall. She looked along the area she could see in the dim, dancing light, but there was no way up the wall that she could tell. She was going to have to stay low and hope for the best.

Ren moved carefully, unsure if at any time, someone might step around a corner, or – if the fates were truly unkind – spot her from above. She moved with low even paces that kept her along the wall and, thankfully, away from any further puddles and piles of mystery meat. ·

Things might be looking up...

Secretly, she knew better. As her eyes crept around the corner, Ren realized she needed to start keeping her mouth shut. Ahead, an area had been carved out of the debris and industrial leavings. Barrels and steel racks and dusty old miscellanea had been thrown outward at all angles from this place and in the center of it, they had built a mountain of death.

At least, that was Ren's guess. In the dim light cast by fires all around the pile, she could see that it was definitely remains. Two figures stood side by side, their arms outstretched, chanting in low unintelligible voices to the mound. The mound shuddered, that same low earthly growl she'd heard earlier. Whatever they were doing was calling forth an earthquake. Ren didn't like this. She thought maybe if she could distract them, it would stop the ritual and the earthquake would cease.

Before she could convince herself to step out of her hiding place, the mound shuddered again and a part rolled down from the top, flopping to the outer ring of the pile. She looked at it with some curiosity until she realized that it was an arm. She looked at the mound with new eyes and those eyes were quick to point out other parts they could recognize now that they had something to look for: fingers, toes, knees, shoulders, hair and a couple of faces; all bloated, slick and melting into one big pile of nastiness.

She shook her head; unable to fathom that this many people could be killed and no one had noticed. There were no warnings, no curfews, and no extra police on the streets. They were just suddenly all dead and no one seemed to care. There had to be dozens of bodies butchered and piled up here. And to what end?

She gripped the wall; uncertain she could handle the darkness suddenly pressing in. *What if Joe was among the victims? What if they hadn't bothered to wait for me?*

Ren was pulled from her thoughts by the

chanting. It had grown louder, more insistent. It sounded like they were issuing commands in an old language, one Ren had never heard. The mountain of gore shook, and in an instant, Ren knew something inside it was clawing its way out. It fumed and huffed from within, a wet thick growl echoed through the room as the pile shifted over it.

An arm emerged, long thin and utterly black, clawing at the ground and trying to pull itself free. Ren thought she recognized the arm and felt the darkness creep in a little tighter, the hope drifted further from her. The hand played as it pulled at the ground and she knew that Joe's hands were not that big, but she had already seen something like that once tonight. They were raising another one of those creatures.

It pulled itself from the bottom of the pile, the rest of the mess collapsing to the side as it shook itself and rose up on wobbling legs, like a baby monster. Its skin shimmered in the wavering light; slick with the leavings of the terrible cocoon it had emerged from. It was definitely not human, and still, very different from Mother Wight's brood. Its musculature was taut, wiry, and wrong in every sense of the word. Ropes of muscle stretched along its limbs; tendons pulled hard at every joint, as if they were the secret to holding it together. It was almost completely folded over on itself, growling and hacking, spitting up on the ground around it.

She felt her head shake slowly, not believing her eyes at all. Somehow they had not only targeted all these people, not only trapped another race of creatures, they had destroyed every one of these being in favor of creating a handful of ugly beasts.

Wasteful doesn't begin to cover this; it's —

She turned around, to the refuse around the hatch she'd crawled up from. Each of these was a withering pile that had been cast over here. She counted the piles and the higher the number, the harder her brain fought to keep its hemispheres together. *Did Tau lie about how many they made? Or did they really try that many times? So much death. So much pointless death.*

She was ripped away from her thoughts by the roar of the beast. It had finally found its lungs. The sound startled Ren to the point of losing her footing and she stumbled, falling clumsily out of her hiding place. She scrambled back, but one of the hooded figures spotted her. She could hear the sick, satisfied smile without having to see it.

"Ah, you found the place!" Tau stepped forward, pushing the hood back. The other figure twisted in her direction, but did not move. It was hunched, shorter than Tau. Small, sharp shoulders poked out of the robe; thin, bony hands were the only feature visible. The person inside this robe was considerably aged, and Ren glared, almost certain she knew who was hiding under the hood. As Tau closed in, the second figure receded from view, though Ren was certain she would face them too. She was almost looking forward to it. "Give me the dagger, and you can have Joe."

Ren stepped into the open, jaw and fists clenched tight. Tau shook his head, making a display of his disappointment.

"I really did expect you to pull it off. Of all people, you were the one I put my faith in to get the job done."

Ren could feel the furnace of anger within her stoking back up. If she could lay a finger on him, he was going to feel every ounce of that fire.

"So sorry to disappoint you. Send Joe home and we can talk about this over tea."

"Talking's done, Ren."

"That's unfortunate, it means you don't have a lot of time left."

He raised an eyebrow, making a show as he turned around the room. "Oh? And what are you going to do? I have an army, remember?" He clapped and called out something in that same unknown language and the beast reared up.

Ren stepped back, kicking at stones beneath her feet. The beast lumbered forward, surprisingly quick. It stopped a few feet shy of mauling her and sniffed at the air, searching. Ren took a step back carefully and started easing her way around objects, trying to put some space between her and it. Tau yelled again and it roared, swiping at the debris around it and sending some of it flying. Ren covered her face and yelped; her footing lost beneath her as she pitched over strewn metal. She gashed her arm on something jagged, though tetanus was the last of her worries at this point.

She pushed herself to her feet and only had a

moment to leap out of the way as the beast came crashing down on where she had just fallen. It tore into the metal, giving her time to get to her feet and cross behind it again.

Tau cried out again, making her spin. Blood spattered from her wound onto the side of one of the burning barrels, sizzling and smoking. Ren leapt the other way as the creature lunged, howling as it tightened its grip around hot metal. It rolled and howled but couldn't get free from the barrel that had fused itself to the beast's flesh. It continued to writhe, dumping coals on itself, until finally, it stopped moving entirely.

She stared at her hand, seeing the blood flow from the wound and amazed that she could hardly feel it. Mother Wight had come through after all. The creature had been hunting her blood, but only when it touched something else.

It smells the blood!

Ren stood up, feeling a tinge of sadness creep up on her. Hell spawn or not, it didn't deserve that. But there would be plenty of time later to sort out feelings and mourn nightmare abominations. Right now, she had eyes for the only man in the room.

His eyes were leveled on her, scowling.

"So you killed a fledgling, good for you." His voice echoed loudly off the high walls and two more rose up from the far end of the warehouse.

"I hope they are smarter than the last one. You did forget to give them the basics, like sight." Like trained beasts, they came when called. They were surprisingly agile for blind creatures, and she could only hope that they were as blind as the last one. They were closing the distance quickly. She looked around, trying to find something to inspire a plan.

"It'll be a pleasure to see that smile fade as you bleed out."

She looked at him and could almost feel the blood dripping a small pool from her fingertips. She blinked slowly, almost wishing she had a better idea, but she knew this was really the only one she needed. Even if it didn't work perfectly, it would buy her some time.

She reached down, grabbing a chunk of jagged concrete in her hand. He looked at her, almost unbelieving as she stood there, and then she lunged. He didn't react for a moment, still lost in surprise. His brain caught up and he surged forward, teeth bared as he growled. But Tau wasn't a fighter; he was a sometimes-thief and some kind of spell-caster. The only thing he had going for him in a fight was his physique, but he didn't know how to use it.

Ren became aware of this as she brought her fist around, connecting in mid-run and taking him off his feet. He scrambled, trying to get away from her, but she was already on top of him, holding him down.

She punched him again, watching his eyes dilate as she let him go, running the ugly stone across her arm, feeling it tear a ragged opening, but the pain was somewhere else. All she felt was the sting of a paper cut as she opened her arm over him.

It might have been a concussion, but as the beasts lumbered down, roaring and growling toward the scene of the fight, he stared almost curiously at her as she pressed an open palm onto his chest, holding him down, the blood spreading across his robes. Rivulets ran up, pooling in the cleft of his collarbone before forking and running down the sides of his neck. She looked up, watching the monsters bear down on her, trying to estimate how many seconds before she needed to move. Calculations were cast aside as Tau's gears found traction and he began fighting against her leverage. She used the moment to her advantage and quickly jumped to her feet, scuttling back.

Tau stumbled, trying to get his feet beneath him. He raised his arms and opened his mouth to speak, but the first one was already on him. He screamed as they pounced, ripping into him. As much as she wanted him to deserve it, Ren looked away and tried to shut out the sounds.

She skirted around the scene, trying to keep her focus ahead of her, looking for an answer to where Joe might be. Again, there was a pang of regret. She should have taken more time. She should have gotten answers, but she pushed the ifs back down. Joe wasn't safe yet, and neither was she, she could question her choices later.

At the far end of the building, she could see doors. They must have been guarding the entrance into the next room. Ren could only hope that it was where they were keeping Joe. Speculation would have to do for now, however. As she stepped forward, one of the creatures behind her bellowed. It huffed and strode forward quickly. She lifted her hand and saw the trail she had left behind her.

Oh no. This is going to be bad.

The second beast was suddenly very interesting in the hunt as well. They shoved and snapped at each other as they followed the trail right up to where Ren had raised her arm up, stopping the trail cold. Or mostly cold. She held her arm tight to her body, trying to staunch the flow, but it was spreading across her chest, and she knew that was going to make her scent stronger. She tried to back away, moving toward the doors. If she could get inside, maybe she could lock them out. Maybe she would be all right.

There was no getting away, though. They raised their faces up, scarred maws sniffing at the air. They wandered together, slowly following the trail, closing in on their prey. She continued to serpentine her way toward the doors, keeping as much of the dwindling distance as she could between them.

One of them bared its teeth, snarling through jagged rows of sharp, yellow horror. It knew she was close, trying to evade capture. It swung its arms forward latching onto nothing but air. It knew as well as she did: they were closing in.

Her head continued to swing from them to the door, back and forth as she tried to continue moving quietly back. She was already fatigued, now she was losing blood and she was getting dizzy from checking and rechecking her path. The factors added up quicker than she anticipated and she lost her footing, tripping on a stray piece of rebar. Her arms flung out defensively and part of her knew that this was it. They would be on top of her before she had time to register the pain from the fall. She hit the ground and rolled as best she could, tucking into a defensive ball.

The sounds were frenzied. They were enraged as they attacked. All Ren could do was listen to the terrifying sounds and wait for it to begin.

She continued to wait so long that she actually had to get up and see why she wasn't dead yet.

They were fighting each other, and Ren realized that she must have splattered one – or both – with her blood when she fell.

You have magical blood. Try to keep some of it inside for next time, would you?

She tried to look away, but it was almost mesmerizing watching these two giants beat on each other.

…But if they run out of blood…

She didn't need to think twice about how that might play out. She turned and ran for it, counting her blessings when the door opened easily. She didn't even stop to secure it; she just kept running down the corridor. She continued down the hall, pushing through another set of doors, where she came into a room that was certainly not like the rest in the building. Where the others were dirty, strewn with debris and viscera, this one was practically immaculate. There were large sconces along the walls lighting the room. In the center of the floor was a circle with an intricate design laid out in the middle of it. It appeared to be drawn in salt, or some powder. There were trunks lined up along the wall, and –

…A bedroom set? Someone lives here?

She started to move slowly toward it when

she noticed a body on the bed. Part of her hesitated momentarily, and then she recognized the soft sleeping face of her heart.

"Joe!" She rushed to her sister's side, shaking her by the shoulders, trying to rouse her from whatever sleep she was in, praying it wasn't the final one. "Joe, come on, time to wake up. We need to go now."

Her eyes fluttered weakly, barely peering through her lashes. Ren couldn't make out a reaction, whether happy or sad, Joe was simply too weak.

"I knew you'd come," Ren had to lean in close to hear her. Joe's voice was barely a whisper, her breathing shallow and slow.

"Of course I did," She tried to hold back the tears, but they were long overdue. "I'm going to take you home now."

This time Joe smiled, her eyes shutting for a long moment. Ren waited for them to open again before she bothered to exhale.

"She's not going to let us go." Joe reached out, taking Ren's hand and holding it as tightly as she could in her weakened state. "You have to leave… before…"

Ren tightened her grip, putting a hand on Joe's cheek, holding her. "Before what, Joe? Don't go. Don't leave me."

"Before it's too late, probably. Isn't that how it goes in all the stories?"

An icy chill crawled down Ren's spine, evaporated by the fire in the pit of her stomach as she stood up. She bent over again, kissing Joe on the head, and then turned to face the rickety old woman.

"Eunice Abernathy. How lovely to see you."

Her robes draped on her, making her look like an old judge. Eunice appeared just as tired and broken as ever, maybe even more so. Her eyes were sunken and sallow, she looked thinner, as if she had stopped eating, but she moved as if she were a teenage athlete having the best day of her life.

"Don't pander to me. I want the knife."

Ren shook her head, shrugging. "That's unfortunate. I don't have it. You should really have taken that up with Mariel."

"I'll be sure to file a formal complaint. I'll write it in your blood after I've drained you dry."

Ren's face screwed, it wasn't a pretty image,

but she hadn't come all this way to simply fail. She clucked her tongue, trying to keep a calm exterior while the rest of her debated running frantically out of here with Joe, versus ripping the old woman to shreds with her bare hands.

"If you don't mind my saying, this all seems like serious lengths to go for William dumping your grandmother."

Ren felt a chill as Eunice cackled. "This isn't about family, child, this is a *personal* vendetta."

Ren shook her head. "You can't be serious."

Her skin drew taut around mouth, wrinkles twisting as they accented her awful broken smile. "Is it beyond comprehension that I could sustain myself for so many years? My magic is all powerful."

Ren had already seen that she might be in a bind, but she hadn't expected to tackle a two hundred year old witch either. Even if she was posturing, it had to take serious power to sustain life. She had to keep Eunice distracted enough so that she wouldn't turn her or Joe into an art project before Ren came up with a way out of this.

"So powerful that it took you two hundred

years to plot your revenge?"

"Without my dagger, it took time to build my power again. I had to do it the hard way, one soul at a time. But I expect after you and your friend, I should have enough power to level Delaney House and everyone in it." Eunice raised her arms outward, as if offering a hug, and Ren was hit full on with a cold blast of air. It startled her, but if she was supposed to quake with fear, it would take more than that. Maybe not much more, admittedly, but she wouldn't surrender to a stiff wind.

She smiled at Eunice and shrugged. "Parlor tricks."

"Stupid girl. You think you're the only special thing on this planet?"

"Well, up till recently… yes?"

"You are far from special. And soon you'll be nothing but a memory."

Ren shook her head. Eunice Abernathy was stalling. She threatened plenty, but hadn't lashed out yet. Maybe she wanted Ren and Joe for collateral. Maybe she was waiting for those awful things to burst through the door.

"The sooner we do this, the sooner I get to

bury you."

Ren's smart mouth got cut off as the wind picked up again and Eunice floated into the air. Her slow shuffling feet were now hovering. Her tired old eyes now glowed with a fierce white light. Ren didn't need a sixth sense to warn her that she might be in a spot of trouble. They stared across the room at each other, the air crackling with energy that made Ren's hair stand up more than usual.

She waited, feeling the tension build between them. The old woman smiled, short jagged teeth greeting Ren again.

"Are you ready to join your sister?" The words echoed in the room, as Eunice floated there and Ren felt her heart punching against her chest. "I'm going to flay you together so you can enjoy each other's suffering."

Every muscle in Ren's body tensed. She had only been trained to defend herself from drunken tough guys; she didn't know anything about fighting magic. If she was going to die, she wanted the last thing she saw to be her hands around Eunice's throat.

"I should have shoved your crotchety bag of

bones down the stairs when I had the chance."

Ren lurched forward, moving as quickly as her muscles would carry her. She put one foot in front of the other, the distance stretching out in front of her with each additional stride. Six paces closer and Eunice hadn't even begun to react. Her arms sliced the air, wishing it were as easy to close the gap between them as flailing her arms. Twelve paces and Eunice did not seem to grasp the situation yet. Only a handful of steps separated her and the wrinkled old neck. She planted her left foot, waiting for the right to catch up, and lunged. Her muscles compacted into a squat and released, ejecting her from the solid ground beneath her feet. She couldn't help but scream, her hands wide and grabbing as she flung herself at Eunice's prone form.

Brilliant light flares from Eunice's eyes, her fists clenched. An invisible force clamps down on Ren's arms, plucking her out of the air, holding her in place. Magic might be powerful, but gravity demands obedience; Ren feels the two struggle as tension builds in her shoulders.

Eunice's fists clenched tighter, fingers working against her palms. Ren would have preferred to ignore the sensation, but every bit of pressure grinding her bones against each other. Even through the pain, she couldn't let the crone get the better of her.

"I think I saw something like this on YouTube once."

The old eyes don't flare, but her mouth twists, scowling as she brings her fists together. Ren tries to be strong, desperate to ignore the crushing sensation that envelopes her, but it's too much. A whimper slips out. She wants to scream, but there's no air, no ability left.

At least I tried, right? That's got to count for something.

Desperately, she tries to look at Joe one last time before everything fades away. Too little and far too late, Ren admits to herself what she had been ignoring this whole time: her feelings for Joe – the non-sisterly variety – running deeper than she could ever have imagined. It was just disappointing that there would be no opportunity to tell Joe.

Joe, who was now upright and leaning heavily on the bed frame, a small kerosene lamp from the bedside table in her shaking hand. There is no clever quip as she throws the lamp in a slow arc. The chimney hits Eunice first, splintering against her skull and cutting her face. The font doesn't break until it hits the ground, rolling down her robe, dousing the fabric with fuel. Her eyes flare momentarily, and Ren collapses, gasping in the moment of reprieve.

Eunice stares hard, holding out a clawed hand to Joe. Her mouth open, ready to fulfill whatever threat she is about to utter, when the lamp crashes. Flames spark up immediately, catching the robe on fire.

She tugs, swatting at the fabric, the fire spreading quickly. Dropping to the ground, she panics, her concentration broken as she tries to rid herself of the flames. Joe collapses, both girls struggling to pull themselves closer to each other as Eunice rails against her own confines. Shedding the black fabric, she pads herself and scowls, smoldering across the room at them.

"I'm going to enjoy sucking your souls out through your eyes."

Ren and Joe are both too weak to care about threats any longer. Their fingers entwined as they fight to pull closer to each other.

Eunice's strange dialect transforms into a strangled cry as she lurches back. Ren turns, seeing what appears to be an arrow piercing Eunice's forearm as she flails. The screams continue, and Ren rolls her head toward other voices shouting their way across the room. Colette is nocking a new arrow into her bowstring with Mariel following close behind; William Delaney's sabre shimmers with dark gore. Ren opens her mouth to call out, to warn them but only a choked whisper escapes her lips.

Eunice clenches her teeth, her arms out as the room erupts in a windstorm. Mariel and Colette can only shield their eyes, but the damage is done. As the wind dies, Colette sweeps the room with her bow, but Eunice is no longer there.

Ren summons every ounce of strength left, tugging her way up Joe's arm, pulling the girl closer and wrapping her in a tight embrace.

"Don't you dare leave me, Joe, don't you leave." The tears come like a waterfall now. Ren's defenses down, her strength gone, the only fight left in her is the one to keep Joe.

"I'm so tired, Ren, I just need to sleep. Five

minutes." Joe smiles softly, her eyes closing slowly.

"No! Stay with me! Stay right here!"

Her eyes flutter slightly, her mouth upturned weakly as she raises a shaky hand to Ren's chest. "I'll stay, right here."

Mariel and Colette rush to Ren and Joe, but Ren hardly notices. Her focus remains solely on Joe and the clammy hand falling away from her chest.

Ren's words mutate into a long, ugly sound full of pain and sadness as Joe's eyes close again.

SEVENTEEN

In her mind, it plays back over and over. Joe closes her eyes, falling limp in Ren's weak arms. Suddenly, Mariel and Colette rush in and separate them, sweeping them both away from this awful place. She relives the moment over and over, as if she could do something different each time, something that might make a difference.

But nothing changes, and the moment continues to repeat.

She sits bolt upright from her dream, immediately regretting the action. Her body is screaming. Every muscle and bone feels cracked and bruised deeply. She collapses back on the bed, wincing, but at least the pain is ebbing back to dull throb.

"I have already told you not to try that again. Twice."

Ren's neck protests, but she manages to turn it far enough to see Mariel sitting in the dim light of the room.

"How did you find us?"

"We call to each other when we are in trouble. Joe called out first, and then you did – very loudly, I might add. We could feel you searching, we knew you would lead us to Joe."

The very mention of the name makes Ren wince.

"Joe. Is she…?"

"In a lot of pain, yes. More than you."

Ren sat up again, ignoring the pain and throwing off the blankets. "She's okay? I need to see her."

Mariel moves close, putting an arm on Ren's shoulder as she attempts to stand, holding her to the bed.

"Relax. You are not going to do Josephine any favors if you get hurt trying to visit her. She is okay, you have only been apart for the day."

Tension falls away, her muscles relaxing.

Mariel wass right: plenty of time to recuperate. But not until she had some answers.

"What the hell has been going on here? Why didn't you tell us?"

She hesitated, pushing strands of her unkempt hair back over her ear. Ren didn't notice until then: Mariel was a mess. There were dark circles under her eyes, a disheveled appearance to her usually neat exterior. A general air of anxiety circled her, even as she tried to play the caring matron. She'd been worried, badly.

"When you are rested – "

"Spill it, Dumbledore."

Her shoulders deflated and she sat next to Ren on the bed.

"Eunice Abernathy has been around a long time. Yes, I knew it was her, but I thought without the dagger, she was without magic. I was wrong; I should have known better. She might live forever if she has the chance to."

"She won't." She winced as she clenched her fist, feeling the pain and letting it throb. "What about the dagger?"

"It is her athame, a ritual dagger. She is powerful, but the dagger would double her power. Anyone who wields the dagger can tap into its magic. But someone with her power can use it to restart her life."

Ren didn't like the sound of that. "Restart?"

"When William," she hesitated at speaking his name. After all this time, she still missed him that much. "Before he met Eunice, she had restarted her life to be young again. Her father Jacob was just a poor stranger who had been charmed into caring for her. He finally managed to fight the charm enough to separate her from the source of her power and took the opportunity, knowing she would kill him for it."

"But William screwed that plan up a little."

She nodded with a small smile. "William was a thoughtful and sometimes foolish man. Eunice had every intention of getting her dagger back from him by charming her way through his defenses. Fortunately, William was also a very private person. He did not know why he was so attracted to the dagger – maybe he had been drawn to the power – but he knew he should keep it safe. She failed at every opportunity, and when he and I met, she knew she had lost him. Then saw her opportunity slipping through her fingers to retrieve the dagger. It drove her crazy. She decided that the only way to get it was to kill us."

"It wasn't a fever then."

She shook her head. Her eyes focused on a dark hole in her heart, remembering everything for just a moment before shutting it away again.

"I suppose for her, it was an easy enough thing to conjure. With us out of the way, she only had to wait for the house to be cleared and she would be complete again."

"But you came back."

"Watching me come back and retake our home upset her, but retaining my youth was the final straw. Her anger has built all this time, and with it her power, but her body is falling apart without the dagger."

"But if her power is still growing, Mother Wight –"

Mariel smiled in the dark, letting out an impressed laugh. "You really have followed the trail to the bitter end. Mother Wight knows the risks. I tried to convince her to abandon the forest; she will not consider it."

"We have to move the athame, dagger,

whatever. And Mother Wight. And we have to track down Eunice. And —" Mariel put a hand on Ren's shoulder and leaned in.

"Right now, you need to rest. There will be time to deal with her. She is off licking her wounds somewhere, and we should do the same."

"But —"

Mariel hushed her again. "And you need to think about what you are going to say to Josephine. She plays tough, but she is such a delicate soul." Ren broke eye contact as she leaned back on the bed, remembering the conversation that more or less led them here.

"She's tougher than you think."

"It is because she loves you, too." Ren heard the words, but they bounced around for a minute before settling, her heart skipping a full beat before redoubling its previous effort.

"How you do you know?"

Mariel patted Ren on the knee, getting up and opening the door. She almost didn't acknowledge the question, but stopped in the doorway, looking back at the girl who had grown so much yet looked much more fragile now than she did when they found her in the morgue.

"You both have that same glow about you. It is the thread that connects you. Now, rest."

* * * *

When she opened her eyes, Ren was surprised to see nothing in the dark of the room. Her whole body ached so much that she expected it to emit a glow that might light up the room. It was a disappointment that it didn't, she could use a distraction from the pain itself.

Against her better judgment – and Mariel's insistence – Ren slowly worked her way out of bed and onto her feet. Her legs shook beneath her, as if they were no longer accustomed to the weight they needed to support. She grit her teeth and tried not to growl as she forced herself to adapt and press on.

You did it once before, you can do this again.

Small steps led her from the side of the bed to the door. Her steps grew bolder as she found walls to help support her. Ren moved from her room to the hall and before she even considered where she was going, she was already standing outside Joe's door.

The moment she realized, her legs stopped shaking. She swayed back and forth gently, threatening to tip forward and push into the room at any moment. Ren closed her eyes and put a palm on the door. Behind her eyelids she could almost see the pale glow: it was like a ribbon of mist moving through the door into the room. She could bet that where it stopped was the same place Joe was sleeping right now.

And then the trembling started. Not in her legs, but in her fingers. Suddenly, doubt was at the forefront of her mind. A thousand creeping questions whispered all at once made her shut her eyes tight and take a step back from the door.

What if Mariel's wrong? What if Joe blames you for all of this? What if she doesn't love you back?

The fear was a sucker punch she couldn't have anticipated. She took another step away, her fingers slipping from the wood of the door to fall listlessly at her side. Was it worth trying only to fail? Could she actually say those words, only to have them fall on deaf ears?

The pain crept back into her body and she felt frail, weak, and alone all at once. Gravity threatened to drag her to the floor, but a sudden noise put everything on hold. The mechanism in the door caught as the knob began to turn. Ren could only stare – part of her wanted to run; the rest of her was paralyzed with fear for any action she might take now.

The door swung slowly of its own volition. In the deeper darkness, Joe stood, leaning against the doorjamb. Her eyes were obscured by unruly bedhead, but Ren found it almost comforting. She couldn't see the emotion in Joe's eyes.

"I didn't mean to wake you." Ren heard her own voice and was surprised how weak it sounded.

"I wasn't sleeping – not much. The pain keeps me up." Ren felt herself nodding as Joe continued. "I heard you out here. I thought you were coming in."

"I –" She started, but the rest caught in her throat. Ren wasn't sure she could go through with it. The doubts were still lingering in the hall with her. "I think I'm beyond exhausted. I'm –"

"No."

It was one word, but it was self-assured. It cut her off mid-thought, and silenced the doubts around her.

"What?"

Joe stepped into the hall, still clinging to the doorframe. "I said no. You don't get to stand outside my door and hesitate. Not after all the hell we've come through. Not when I am standing right here in front of you."

The blood rushed to Ren's face. She shut her eyes. She wanted to speak, but even with the doubt cast aside, she was overwhelmed. She took a deep breath, her hand coming to her mouth.

"I wasn't all there the night you saved me – the first time – but I heard you." Ren's eyes opened as Joe took her hand, placing it over her heart. "You already have my heart, Ren. You don't need to ask."

The tears pushed forth: happy tears crowding out fearful tears as they all fell together. Ren's fingers fumbled, finally grasping enough of Joe to pull her in tight. They folded into an embrace of limbs. Ren pressed her lips to Joe's cheek; sobbing as she let go of all the pain and fear she'd felt for Joe and let the relief and delight crowd in.

"I love you, I love you, I love you." Ren forced the words through the heavy emotions. "I was so scared. Scared that you'd die before I could tell you, and scared that you wouldn't say it back, and –"

Joe put a finger to Ren's lips. Her cheeks shimmered with tears, but her smile shone brighter.

"Shh. I love you, Ren. Of course I do."

Ren was flush with a tide of emotions; feeling like Joe might be the only thing keeping her from collapsing now. "I'm sorry I didn't say it sooner. I'm sorry th–"

Joe hushed her again.

"Shut your stupid face and kiss me."

EIGHTEEN

A month passed and though Ren and Joe had both recovered from most of their injuries, they still took turns waking up in cold sweats in the middle of the night, screaming and fighting the shadows. Mariel and Colette spoke casually of selling the other houses and bringing everyone back under one roof. Ren wasn't sure if that would be good or bad. There were eight other sisters she didn't know and, while she could trust Joe's judgment on some of them, there no telling how she would get along with all of them. She also had no idea if that would work for or against them as far as Eunice was concerned. She was still out there, and she would come after them again. Was a dozen bustling supernaturals under one roof a benefit or a liability? She tried to steer the conversations back to house shuffles, where members would move to different houses periodically, but Mariel seemed distracted. Some days she was all-in and ready to move forward with a new strategy, other days, she looked like there was trouble brewing already. Both Joe and Ren mentioned it, but Mariel brushed concerns aside, expressing her own concern about their progress back to full health.

Time and a regular work schedule brought most things back to an even keel. Maintaining the showrooms had become something Ren actually looked forward to. She understood now that the routine was what kept them sane through the passing years. It gave them something to depend on, no matter how crazy things got. She was learning to appreciate that, and she was going to hold onto it. As tightly as necessary.

She had just finished another day in the ordinary world, noting to herself how almost normal her body felt again. It was close to being fully healed. She might even be able to race up a flight of stairs again without shooting pains in her ribs, but she wasn't going to push it just yet.

She was approaching the front entrance, ready to begin locking up for the day when it burst open. A hooded figure stepped into the room and for a moment, Ren had the keen inspiration to grab the nearest heavy object and bludgeon it, just for old time's sake. Before she could actually do that though, she had to grab the nearest structural support and hold on as the room closed in around her. She shut her eyes tight and took a deep breath, fighting the anxiety back down.

"Are you okay?" The voice was young and soft. It tugged at her, pulling her away from the darkness.

"I'll be fine. You startled me, that's all."

"I'm sorry. I was hoping to get here before you closed for the evening."

She took another deep breath, opening her eyes. "I'm just closing up for the night, actually. But if you'd like to come back tomorrow…"

"I'd prefer not, honestly. It's been hard enough to find my way here."

Ren's skin prickled and she felt her muscles tense. It was possible she was being paranoid, but she'd rather be ready than caught off guard. She looked closer at the girl. Her hood was still up, which did nothing to ease frayed nerves. Her hands were tucked deep into the pockets of a grey pea coat. She wore a skirt with leggings under it, and leather boots. If she was a danger, she was an exceptionally fashionable one.

"I've been looking for someone, and the trail went cold here." She pulled her hands from her pockets, reaching up and pushing back the hood. Ren's muscles were taut, and she was ready to defend herself, but as the hood fell away, she found herself completely disarmed by what her eyes beheld.

The girl appeared to be very nervous, trying to gauge Ren's reaction as she stood there. The stare down – a silent contest that neither of them had consciously entered – had never officially begun between them, so neither knew how to end it, adding an enormous weight to the room.

"I would appreciate it very much if you said something right now. *Anything*, in fact."

Ren couldn't stop staring. The room skewed slightly as Ren tried to will the blood back into her brain. This girl had all the same features, right down to the furry skin, as Tau. Her ears were mostly obscured, but Ren could see the points sticking out, parting her hair on the sides. Her eyes were softer than his, a lush green-blue. But she was definitely his sister.

She began to look sheepish, as if she might have picked the wrong person to reveal herself to. She threaded her fingers, fidgeting nervously. Ren swallowed, her throat had gone dry, but she managed to choke out a single word.

"Panya?"

Her ears perked and her large eyes widened as she bounced.

"You've met Tau! Oh please, tell me where I can find him! I've been so worried!"

* * * *

Ren and Joe took turns staring at Panya from across the coffee table. The family resemblance was uncanny, though they agreed that the characteristics lent themselves better to women than they did men. Her bangs were pointed, mimicking the natural angle of her brow. The rest of her hair was in a bob. The whole thing was dyed a deep shade of burgundy, which played well off her pale complexion. She wore the dark eyeliner of rebellious teens the world around, which did her no favors as her mascara spread woefully as she teared up.

Ren sat her down and brought her a cup of tea before telling her most of the story about Tau. Joe joined in unintentionally, hearing the cries and coming to see the commotion. She sat in and joined them for the rest of the conversation.

They decided not to tell her what they actually knew about Tau. That he had been a thief, a liar, and that he had met his end at the hand of the same dark forces he tried to control. Instead, they filled in a glorified version of the Tau they had known: that he had been threatened to assist some very bad people, or they would hurt his sister. They did tell her that he met his end in the warehouse, where they believed Panya was being held.

For her part, she had never known where Tau had gone off to, only that he had been gone for more than a year and she feared the worst. It was easy to follow rumors of a strange looking man as he wandered the continent, but when they ended here, she didn't know what that meant.

Ren and Joe struggled to find other things to tell her. In the short time they had known Tau, he hadn't offered a lot of personal information. Instead, they let her fill in the gaps, giving her a chance to talk about herself, her family, Tau, and in turn, they told her about their own family. They talked late into the night, introducing Colette when she finally came out to say good night. Mariel had declined to introduce herself, but she would be around in the morning.

They gave her some pillows and a quilted blanket, leaving her to the couch. They agreed as a group that she could figure out her next move after she got a good night's sleep.

* * * *

Ren woke with a jolt; sweat prickling her forehead and her heart racing in her chest. In her dreams, she saw those awful creatures again, all muscle and horror. She wondered if any of them were still alive out there and how many of them there might be.

She didn't have much time to think about it. A shrill voice ripped through the silence, a cry from downstairs. Instinct pulled Ren out of bed and into action. She darted out the door and charged down the stairs. There was another cry from the couch as Ren rushed forward in the darkness.

"It's alright, it's just me – Ren." She slowed as she saw Panya scrambling away from her. They were both panting, out of breath for their own reasons. "I heard a scream. You alright?"

"Yes. Well, no." She took a breath. "It was a nightmare. I've been having them since Tau disappeared. It's childish, I know." Ren sat down beside her.

"No, there's nothing childish about it. I've had them a lot lately, since Tau…" Panya looked up a Ren, her eyes glittering with tears in the darkness. "Sometimes, bad things happen, and we don't know how to cope, so we have nightmares."

She nodded, the tears coming harder, and leaned into Ren, wrapping her arms around Ren's waist and sobbing into her lap. Ren cradled the young girl. She wanted so much to comfort

Panya, but Ren was caught between two Taus – the one she fought and the one Panya mourned.

"I miss him so much. I just don't know what I am going to do without him."

"You're going to live. You'll find a way, I promise."

Panya squeezed Ren tighter, sniffling, the tears subsiding and her breathing balancing itself.

"At least I know he didn't die afraid and alone. Thank you for being there with him."

Ren sat in the darkness, caressing the broken girl to sleep as the guilt prodded at her, tugging at her conscience. She waited for Panya's breath to steady and deepen, signifying her steady drift into sleep. There was a moment, when that was exactly how she wished it would have happened. She understood that people make bad decisions sometimes, especially when they have good intentions. She forced herself to believe that's exactly what it was: the best of intentions. She tried to push the rest of her memories aside and just live with the one that his sister believed.

The Delaneys will return.

A WORD FROM THE AUTHOR

Readers are an author's lifeblood. They bring reviews, which bring more attention – and more readers – and encourage us to do what we do: keep writing. So, if you enjoyed this book – or, really, any book at all – please review it on all of your favorite merchant and social media sites. Or anywhere you can find it. If you can't find it somewhere, ask them to carry it.

If you would like to keep in touch, you can find me at:

www.happierthoughts.com

Most importantly though: Thank you – for being a reader, and for taking a chance on my work. I hope you enjoyed reading this as much as I enjoyed creating it.

Andy

ACKNOWLEDGEMENTS

Bailey Lockwood threatened me with death and dismemberment (in no particular order) to ensure the triumphant launch of this adventure. I cherish her dedication as an editor, a fan, and a friend. These things I do could not be accomplished without her.

You can learn more about her amazing work at:

www.justduckyediting.com

Brian Ritson went beyond the call with this cover, plucking the idea directly from my head and putting it into visual medium with skills akin to sorcery. He is a wonderful and talented artist and I am lucky to call him my friend.

You can view his portfolio at:

brianritson.wixsite.com/mysite

ABOUT THE AUTHOR

Andy Lockwood is a writer, artist, dreamer, and horror enthusiast. He got his start in screenwriting and filmmaking, where he rekindled his obsessive love of storytelling.

He is the author of three novels: *Empty Hallways*, *House of Thirteen*, and *Threshold*; a 12-part serial, *At Calendar's End*, and is a contributor to various horror anthologies. He is always at work on another piece of writing, whether it is a novel, a story, or something else entirely. When not lashed to the keyboard, he buys books he does not have time to read, and delves into mediums he has no time to fully explore, but dabbles in them anyway.

He lives in Michigan with his amazingly talented and entirely-too-supportive wife, a brood of cats, and a misguided idea of what it means to be an adult. More information about his work is neglectfully curated at his website:

www.happierthoughts.com